Straight

Face

Brandon Wallace

GREEN BRIDGE
• PRESS •

Visit at thegaychristian.com

Published in the United States by Green Bridge Press, LLC. GREEN BRIDGE PRESS, LLC. and colophon are registered trademarks of Green Bridge Press, LLC

Library of Congress Cataloging-in-Publication Data
Wallace, Brandon
Straight-Face / by Brandon Wallace p. cm.
ISBN 9780983567752 (alk. paper)
LCCN 2014950165
1. Biography & Autobiography : Personal Memoirs. 2. Religion : Christian Life - Social Issues. 3. Biography & Autobiography / LGBT.

Printed in the United States of America.

First Edition - Revised (12/18/14)

Book & Cover Design by Shelda Edwards

Wallace, Brandon (2014-12-16). *Straight-Face*. Green Bridge Press.

Acknowledgements

To my parents: you mean the world to me. You taught me to be the man I am today, and I am eternally grateful.

Allan, my brother, you are my hero, and you always will be. We're not only brothers; we are the greatest of friends. I will always cherish that.

To Kirstyn, my best friend, and all of the members of Kehila that stuck with me through it all: your friendship is always reliable, and I know that you will always be by my side.

To the **friends** I have made since the day I came out, especially Bud, Dan, Rachel, and Andrew: you have allowed me to follow my dreams and helped make this possible by pushing me toward it.

To Tim: publishing this book has formed a friendship that I am ever grateful for, and I look forward to the years of working alongside you. Thank you for helping make a dream come true.

To Connie, my protector: thank you for helping lead me away from bondage and pushing me into the freedom of Christ. Thank you for being my second momma, and thank you for being a rock during the hardest time of my life.

Father Joseph, my priest and my friend, thank you for helping me get to the place I am today, and thank you for leading me on my current path.

To Connor: I'm glad we had the time together that we had, and thank you for helping me grow into the person I am today.

In early 2014, as I prepared this book for publication, I ran an IndieGoGo campaign to help raise funds to promote the book. I was blown away by how fast people came to my aid. It gave me hope and faith that this really is a story that God can use for his benefit, and I have made many friends through the process. Below is a list of those who helped make this book possible:

Sandie Weinrauch
Jaime Vidal
Gary Oliver
Steve Schmidt
Daniel Parker
Robert Rogers
Marty Carney
Brittany Edwards
Ashton Gilstrap
Preston Blair
Daniel Tidwell
Terry White
Daniel Bergfalk
Robert Lofgren
Amy Stevlingson
Paul Deeming

Barbara Vann
Joy Heath
Valery Fischer
Dan Brooks
John House
Melissa Cooper
Cecily Long
Jacob Steele
Jennifer Garner
Richard Marx
Debra Hudson
Michael Watt
Sarah Wofford
Kirsty Wyatt
Juan Fuentes
The many anonymous donors

"Hope sings from the pages of Brandon Wallace's story, which is a beautiful accomplishment considering *Straight-Face* isn't always a happy tale. Still, even as Wallace retells the most difficult parts about being a Christian gay man serving in ministry, he details this journey with maturity, wit, confidence, and joy. Yet, despite the struggle and hardships that Wallace endured, *Straight-Face* is a hopeful tale, a story about a man finding life, God, and the freedom to be gay."

-Matthew Paul Turner, Our Big Great Awmerican God

"What a gripping story - so refreshingly honest! Brandon Wallace captures the angst and inner struggle in the mind of a gay son in a religious environment. Every parent of a gay son or daughter should read this story! It will change your outlook on this tough subject!"

- Grace McLaren

"Brandon Wallace has successfully challenged us to take off our masks, to embrace our authentic selves, and for that we all owe him thanks."

-Timothy Kurek, The Cross in the Closet

For all of those who are
still stuck behind their masks

Table of Contents

Foreword

Brandon Wallace is my hero. Not because he is superhuman, but because he is human.

Brandon is raw and unabashedly honest. In the past three years, I have watched him grow into himself and into his faith in ways that astound me. You see, Brandon is the man that could have changed it all for me early on in life. Growing up in a strict, conservative Christian home, I never knew that there were Brandon's out there. If I had access to his story back then, it may have saved me from years of living as a modern-day Pharisee.

Many books have come out in recent years that make the case for a more progressive theological perspective about homosexuality, but none have so shocked me in their transparency. Where most seem to hide behind smoothed edges and dulled details, *Straight-Face* is honest; it is so honest that it sometimes made me uncomfortable. It didn't make me uncomfortable because it offended me, but rather because in reading this book, I see that Brandon is setting an example that all of us should follow: never hide your beautiful face behind a mask. Never allow the world to oppress you or diminish you. Always be who you are and be thankful for the bumps in the road that build character. Brandon's road has been full of potholes, speed bumps, and hairpin turns. But sometimes, the bumpiest roads are the most beautiful. Brandon's life and heart are definitely beautiful.

It is my hope that this book and Brandon's story will challenge your preconceived notions about God, and encourage you to allow His infinite grace, which surpasses all knowledge, to root you in authentically unconditional love. Not just unconditional love of others, but also of yourself, your true self - the self we so often hide behind our own masks in order to appease the wrong people. It is also my hope that this story will cause you to wrestle with your own salvation, and in looking at Brandon as an example, you will feel a renewed sense of hope that God simply loves you just as you are, and not as you believe you should be.

Are you ready to look behind your mask?

- Timothy Kurek,
author of *The Cross in the Closet*

Prologue

I actually didn't intend to write a book. I was simply wanting a cathartic outlet for everything I was feeling inside. In early 2012, I had just come out of the closet as a gay man. I had packed up and moved to Memphis, Tennessee, in an attempt to escape the place I called home for the many years prior. I was tired, confused, scared, and alone. I didn't know what to do. Writing was the only outlet that I had.

I sat down at a coffee shop originally intending to write a blog post just to help others understand my story. I had left behind hundreds of confused people at the church in which I was ministering, and I wanted them to simply get a glimpse at my side of the story, so as to help them get a better understanding of why I chose to finally come out of the closet.

After writing profusely, I looked up to realize that hours had passed, and I had already written thousands of words. Considering I was in between jobs, I had plenty of free time; so, the following day,

I went back to that coffee shop and wrote even more. This continued day after day, until a week later, I had this entire book written. The way each word poured out of me, I could tell that I needed this release of emotion. Even if no one else read the words I had written, it was still therapy for me.

After the week was finished and the book was written, I tucked it away on my hard drive without really thinking much more about it. Like I said, I felt it was more for me than anyone else, anyway.

Some time passed, and I shared my writing with a couple of people. They persisted that this was a story that needed to be heard, and as much as I didn't believe them, I went ahead and shared it with my friend in publishing. I received a message just days later reaffirming what my friends had told me. He told me that this was a book that needed to be published, because it was a story that should be shared.

My editor decided she didn't want to edit much of the content, because from the outset, we felt it was important to hold true to the emotions and thoughts that were going through me during that tumultuous season of my life. (However, she did a wonderful job proof editing for me!) Today, things have definitely gotten better. It has been a beautiful journey, and it's a journey that I know still has a long way to go. With this book, however, I share with you my story as authentically as I can. A few names and details have been changed to protect people's identities, but I believe it's enough detail to help you get a full grasp of the journey thus far.

I am still living in Memphis, and life definitely takes its toll sometimes. But, I wouldn't change a thing about where God has brought me. Even though it was one of the worst seasons of my life, it was also one of the most beautiful seasons of my life, because through my journey, I learned the intensity of God's love, the beauty of God's freedom, and the power of authenticity.

We Wear the Mask
BY PAUL LAURENCE DUNBAR

We wear the mask that grins and lies,
It hides our cheeks and shades our eyes,—
This debt we pay to human guile;
With torn and bleeding hearts we smile,
     And mouth with myriad subtleties.

Why should the world be over-wise,
In counting all our tears and sighs?
Nay, let them only see us, while
     We wear the mask.

We smile, but, O great Christ, our cries
To thee from tortured souls arise.
We sing, but oh the clay is vile
Beneath our feet, and long the mile;
But let the world dream otherwise,
     We wear the mask!

Chapter One

I have never remembered Jonesboro being so dark. As I lay my head against the passenger's side window, I see the lights fly past me as fast as the last few months - all a blur.

I can't believe it has come to this, I think to myself.

It is almost midnight as Connie Waters, an ex-Methodist minister who has become my second mother, whips the SUV into the driveway of the old duplex apartment. The place that I called my home just a few days ago now looks like a dungeon in the sly moonlight.

As we step out of the vehicle, my now ex-roommate and his girlfriend rush through the door to give me a hug. It has been less than a week since I've seen them, but it has felt like much longer. Pulling away from their embrace, I notice the tears in their eyes.

Kirstyn, my best friend, rushes through the door and grabs ahold of me. Looking toward the door, I now realize that she, as well as three of my closest friends are here, waiting for me. But there is no time to waste.

We know we need to get inside quickly.

There have been too many threats received over the last few days for me to be seen outside. This was the reason Connie and I waited until the middle of the night to return to this sleepy town. Passions and tensions are running high, and as of right now, the prodigal son of this community has returned home - but in this case, he wasn't welcomed with a father's embrace.

It's only been six days since I left the Baptist church I was working for, and only four days since I was outted as gay.

Four days, I think. It's felt like four years.

These ninety-six hours have left me with no sleep, not much food, and so many hate-filled text messages and phone calls that I had to change my number.

As we step into the apartment, my friends have my belongings bagged up and ready to move. We each grab bags and furniture and hurl them into Connie's SUV, making sure not to make too much of a scene. We aren't sure how serious the threats are, but we don't want to take any chances.

Finally, the SUV is loaded down and we lock ourselves inside the duplex. I gaze at everyone circled around the dark living room. They look lost. I feel lost. Everyone can tell that this last week has been grueling for me physically, emotionally, and spiritually.

But, I can also tell their hearts have been broken, too. Here I stand before them, their minister and their friend, and I am having to run away from my own hometown. For the last three years, the eight of us have become closer than brothers and sisters as we sat each week in Bible study, devouring Scripture, and coming to know God in a way we never thought imaginable. Yet, it was the people of our very own

"Bible-believing" church that were threatening that they "better not ever see me out in the street."

I look at each one of them as we sit in silence for those few moments. We feel as lost as the disciples in the Upper Room after Jesus' ascension.

What now? What do we do? Are we safe? What comes next?

The questions run through each of our heads. The problem is that none of us have any answers. My friends feel cut off from their own families for simply calling me friend, and God has given me nothing but silence in my loud cries for answers.

Silence.

The silence is so loud.

"Well," I say quietly as I let out a sigh, "here we are."

I take a seat on the couch arm beside my best friend as she hugs me, wiping a tear from her eye.

"Everything is out in the open now," I continue, "and there is not much more we can do except try to out-love them. I know it doesn't sound easy, and right now all of us want nothing more than to be bitter and return the hate with hate. But, that's not an option at this point. All we can do is ride it out, have each other's back, and love those that don't love us. It's game on."

We hug and pray for one another, then Connie and I head for the SUV. We jump in, and pull out of the driveway as we wave goodbye to everyone.

I let out a huge sigh of relief that we made it out of town with no problems.

"How are you feeling?" Connie asks, with that Southern, motherly tone that she uses so well.

There's a question for the ages, I think.

Honestly, I didn't know how to respond. Everything I had ever known has now changed.

"It's all…different." I finally say with a shrug.

"Honey, this is just the beginning."

I slump against the window once again, hoping she's right, as I watch my hometown disappear behind me in the passenger-side mirror.

———————————

Even though I'm no longer serving full-time in a church, I do consider myself a minister of sorts. I may have left that particular church, but that doesn't mean my calling has changed. The look in my friends' eyes as I pulled away from that duplex said that this was far from over. There is still plenty of work that needs to be done, and just because one group of Christians rejects me, that does not mean Christ does.

I never really knew what kind of minister I was going to be, or even what that really meant. But I knew I wanted to do it. I remember being seven years old, preaching to an empty living room. My dad owned a huge Rainbow Bible, which color-coded everything for easy reference. I would hold that gigantic Bible in my little seven-year old hands, and scream to the couch and recliner about God's anger, and how they needed mercy upon their sinful furniture souls.

I think the chair was saved that day, but the recliner was too stubborn.

The problem was that being a minister was not the only thing I've known since I was about seven. The other thing I've known is that I am gay. Granted, I had no word for it at the time, but I knew something was different.

I remember being on the playground in a town near where I grew up. A little girl was there, chasing me around and flirting like little girls do. She would chase me around the monkey bars, and then I would escape to the swings. She would come over to the swings, and I'd escape to the monkey bars.

Somehow, my little stalker cornered me in a playhouse under the slide. There was only one exit, and she had that blocked.

"I like you," said the little Siren in Training. "Do you like me, too?"

I didn't even know this chick! All I knew was that she freaked me out.

"I don't know." I said, ambivalently, as I tried to formulate my escape plan.

That's when it happened.

She gave me those eyes. You know the ones. They squint a little bit, and then follow with a smirk, followed by the puckering up of lips.

What is she doing?

She began to lean in closer with those puckered lips and it finally dawned on me what she was doing: she was going to kiss me!

"I think my mom is calling me!" I yelled as I bolted for the playhouse door.

Luckily, her eyes were closed so I could slip by her. It was the oldest trick in the book, but I didn't have time to question whether it would work or not. I just knew I had to get out from under that slide.

Now, this situation is not all that uncommon for seven year olds, but what I remember next is uncommon, I presume. I remember running away from that Evil Slide of Seduction and seeing a boy about my age run by me.

Hmm, now if he wanted to kiss me, I would let him, I thought.

At the time, I didn't even give this a second guess. It was just a fleeting thought. Besides, I didn't have time to stop and philosophize about what I was thinking and feeling. I was too busy getting away from the Siren of the Slides.

If there's one thing I've learned over the last few years, it's that religion isn't what the gospel of Jesus Christ is about. As a matter of fact, it's almost in complete opposition to the gospel.

Now, I know the word "religion" holds a wide array of meanings for different people. For some people, religion means their church and all of the rituals involved. For others, it means negativity and war. When I say "religion," however, I mean the part that replaces faith. All of the bells and whistles of religion are not a bad thing; the church is not a bad thing. But, when someone makes religion an idol for which they snuff out what God is trying to do, or to hide the true, living God himself, that's when things go sour.

This was a major part of the Gospel of Jesus Christ. He stood in opposition to the religious leaders of his time, the Pharisees, because they were trying to use religion to parade around town and show greatness. They used their religion to condemn other people for not being the same way. That is religion in its ugliest form. That is the type of religion that Jesus stood against.

Religion leads to death; the Gospel leads to life.

Real life. True life. Abundant life.

Really, that's what my story has been about: the gospel's leading me to real life - the gospel's leading me away from religion.

Being gay and being in the evangelical church takes a toll on your real life, because, well, real life doesn't exist. You play a character. You play someone else. Bad religion kills off who you are - or, at the least, silences you - and replaces you with a cookie-cutter version of who you are told you are supposed to be. It's even in the word. Many scholars even believe that our English word "religion" is derived from the latin *religare*, which literally means, "to bind up." That's exactly what corrupt religion does. It binds us up and puts us in bondage to whatever it is our religion says.

The gospel does something different, though. The gospel, which literally means "good news," calls you right where you are, just as you are, to come and be a part of something much bigger. The gospel of Jesus Christ calls you to bring yourself - your true self - to the kingdom of God.

This is not something I learned overnight.

As a matter of fact, it took me a really long time to come to this conclusion, and although it was a wild and bumpy ride, I wouldn't change a thing.

In this scary, dark, lonely car ride to my new home, I am right where I need to be, and let's be honest: when it comes to the callings of God, he usually leads us to places that are scary, dark, and lonely. He calls us into hard situations, just so something beautiful can grow out of it.

Now, don't get me wrong, I'm not saying all parts of religion are bad. Some religious people do really great things. They feed people, they house people, they help people with addictions. To be totally honest, I personally love religion. Sometimes, it feels like more of a love/hate relationship, but it is deeply engrained within me.

I see a beauty in religion that other people may not see.

It's sort of like a friend of mine who has an old, worn-out truck. He loves that old truck, and when he looks at it, his face shines and he smiles; he sees a beautiful stallion glimmering in the wind. When I look at it, though, I see a hunk of metal that could probably be used for scraps. When it comes to religion, I am more like my friend with his truck. I derive so much from it, and feel at home within it, even though I know there are so many things wrong with it.

I love the tribal-style worship setting of the contemporary, evangelical church.

I love the depth and the solemnity of the liturgical, mainline denominations.

I love baptisms, the communion, and even the organ.

I love just being a part of it.

But as much as I love being a part of it, I got to experience first-hand the ugly side of religion. I got a hands-on observation of just how much religion can bind us up and keep us from true life.

My story is one of Jesus calling me out of my religion - the religion that I loved and held so close to my heart - so that I could live.

He asked me to let go of it so that I could follow Him, and that's exactly what I did.

But I didn't let it go without a fight.

Chapter Two

Anyone who knows me knows that I am a huge Bob Dylan fan.

My passion for Dylan's music started when I thirteen and was just beginning to learn to play the guitar. Mrs. Lopez, an old hippie lady who lived next door, introduced me to his rendition of "Mr. Bojangles," and I was hooked instantly. I would sit and listen to him for hours as I tried to strum along on my guitar. To this day, just listening to Bob Dylan's music takes me back home.

As with a lot of people, I'm not a Dylan fan because of his voice, though. What draws me to Dylan are the words he sings. He has a rare ability to write powerful phrases and words that can cut through your soul and create an existential crisis.

He's an absolute genius.

In an interview in May of 1965, Dylan said, "All I can do is be me — whoever that is."

While that phrase captures where I currently am in life, it has not always been the case. As it is with many gay people, most of my life has been about running away from discovering who I really am.

I've always had a deep conviction to be true to myself, and to what I believe, and for most of my life, as with most evangelical Christians, I believed that being gay was an abomination to God. I believed that if a person was homosexual, then odds were that God did not much care for them. That person was probably going to end up spending eternity in Hell.

It was odd theology for someone with same-sex attraction, but that's why it was important for me to believe that I wasn't really gay. But, this theology was all that I knew.

I grew up in Arkansas, about an hour northeast of Memphis, Tennessee. I resided in the heart of Bible Belt America, and conservative Christianity was pretty much the only flavor of religion. My family began going to a rural Baptist church of about thirty to forty people when I was five years old.

As with most conservative, rural, Baptist churches, on Sundays you mainly heard sermons about God's wrath, your sin, and how you needed to be saved by the sacrifice of Jesus Christ if you didn't want to burn in Hell for eternity.

At five years old, I didn't really know what the words "wrath," "sin," or "sacrifice" meant, but I knew I didn't want to burn forever without end. Sunday after Sunday, I heard about the need to "be saved," and I couldn't take it anymore. Things started to click, and I realized what I needed to do. On a hot Sunday in July, as the pianist (who happened to be my aunt) began playing "Just As I Am" on the piano, I walked up the aisle to the preacher at the altar, who was wiping beads of sweat off of his burly forehead.

He was a nice man, but very big. Even though he was much

bigger than me, I remember how comfortable and safe I felt with him. For me, at five years old, he was the spokesperson for God. There was an air of respect for this man, as well as great fear.

He smiled at me as he knelt down on one knee so he could be closer to me, his breathing still heavy and fast from the fiery sermon.

"What can I do for you, son?" he asked in his deep Southern drawl.

"I...I...uh," I looked at my dad to make sure I was at the right spot. He smiled at me from the pew and gave me the nod to go ahead with what I was doing.

"I want to be saved!" I finally got it out.

Just being up at the front of the church with the preacher was nerve-wracking. I wasn't totally sure what was going on here, but I knew it would be worth it to not burn in Hell for all of eternity.

"Well, that is great!" the preacher said with a smile on his face, wiping his forehead, "Let me ask you a couple of questions."

Questions? I thought, as the song rolled into the fourth verse, and the congregation sang. *This guy has questions? I don't know any answers! I just know I don't want to burn forever!*

"Do you know who Jesus is?" he asked, still smiling.

"God's son." I replied. That was easy. I learned that in Sunday school. I hope they are all this easy..

"That's exactly right," he said, "and do you know what he did for you?"

Oh, I know this one, too, I thought.

"He died on the cross so I can go to Heaven."

His smile grew.

"Yes!" he exclaimed.

I must have passed the test.

11

"So, I want you to repeat this prayer after me, but you really have to mean it. Ok?"

"Ok." I said back, still unsure, but willing.

He began the prayer, two or three words at a time. I followed along, squinting my eyes and praying as hard as I could so that God would know that I really meant it.

"Jesus," I prayed, "I know that I'm a sinner. I know I need you to save my soul from Hell. I'm sorry for my sin, and I ask that you come into my heart and save me. In Jesus' name I pray, Amen."

And just like that, I was saved. Well, that's what the preacher told me, anyway.

I wasn't exactly sure how this all worked, but my preacher said I was good to go, so I took his word for it.

Not soon after that in another sermon, however, I was told that if I kept on sinning, it might mean that I was not really saved, which meant I could still go to Hell. Apparently, when I "got saved," I was signing a lifelong contract agreeing to try and never sin again to prove that I actually was saved. I felt like a bait-and-switch had occurred, but it was too late. I had already signed up, and I still did not want to burn for eternity, so I gave in.

As I grew older and attended Sunday school, I began to grasp a lot more though, and my faith became very important to me. I was taught that it was my duty to go out and tell the world about Jesus so that they, too, wouldn't burn in Hell for all eternity. Saving people was the ultimate purpose in this life, and I was as excited as the next guy about being a part of it. I mean, hey, I liked people. I didn't want them to burn.

By the time I had turned seven years old, I knew only a few things: 1) I was saved, 2) It was my duty to tell other people that they were sinners and were going to burn in Hell if they didn't accept Jesus as their Lord and Savior, and 3) I didn't like it when little girls tried to kiss me.

It wasn't a lot, but little did I know, those three things were going to shape the rest of my life.

———————

Even though I have that vivid memory from the playground at age seven and can see the traces of my homosexuality at a young age, at the time, I thought nothing about it. I knew nothing about sex, or "being gay or straight," or anything of that nature.

That all changed a short few years later, however.

Some pretty big things happened in the year 1998: human cloning was outlawed in Europe, the winter Olympics were being held in Japan, Bear Grylls became the youngest man to climb Mount Everest, and our family got our first computer with internet.

I was always pretty tech savvy. I think it was part of being a child of the nineties. At ten years old, I was already far more advanced than my parents when it came to computers. I was the one that set the computer up, the one that installed AOL, and often times, the one that talked to tech support when my dad would get frustrated and hand me the phone.

It also meant that my parents had no idea what all was out there on the World Wide Web, either.

It didn't take me long before I discovered the dark side of the Internet.

"You can find naked people online!" my older cousin told me. He was thirteen, and stayed at our house a lot. Since I was only ten, he was like a hero to me.

"Really?"

That was the only reply I had because, quite honestly, I couldn't really figure out why anybody would want to sit and look at pictures of naked people. It sounded kind of gross.

"Yeah, I've heard people at school talk about it. It's free and everything."

"That's weird," I said, still pretty confused.

"No, it's not weird," he said, with an air of confidence. "You'll grow up and understand one day."

Well, I couldn't let him think that I was too immature! Besides, the thought sort of intrigued me a little. I still wasn't sure why people would want to look at other people naked, but for curiosity sake, it sounded interesting enough to at least check it out.

That night I waited until everyone went to bed, and then I began dialing the internet. The modem rang out in all of its screeching glory, and I was sure my parents were going to hear it and wake up. The computer was on the other side of the house from the bedrooms, but the modem was so darn loud I just knew I was going to get caught. After repeatedly checking the hallway for any signs of consciousness, I finally heard my dad's loud snore coming from the bedroom. I sighed a sigh of relief and then logged on to AOL. I didn't really know where to start, so I just searched for "naked people." I don't remember much about what I saw, but I do remember one thing: I was confused.

I didn't understand why this was so fun, but it was exhilarating. It made my body do things that my body had never done before, and this intrigued me even more. I was still tolerably confused, but it didn't take long to put two and two together.

After a few videos and many pictures, I began to figure things out, and it all started making sense.

I had discovered sex.

There was no going back.

The thing that I found more confusing than anything, though, was that I could care less if women were even on the screen. I knew that it was the guys that I liked watching, and they were the ones that were making my body quiver and my heart beat faster.

What did this mean?

Shouldn't it have been the women getting me excited? I mean, from what I had seen so far, whatever those women were doing sure seemed to work for those men! But I just couldn't take my eyes off of the men. It was part admiration, part something-else-I-didn't-have-a-name-for-yet. I was enamored with watching them, and studying their bodies, their moves, their emotions.

The men made me excited, and that muddied my ten-year old mind. I knew this was something that wasn't "normal," because of how I had heard older boys talk. So, I conceded that I just wouldn't tell anyone about this - even my older cousin.

Finally, I closed it all out, cleared my history, and went to bed.

Immense guilt clouded my mind as I crawled my shaking ten-year-old body into bed. Confusion and distress settled in for the night.

What was I doing? What would God think about this?

I was scared.

I mean, I was really scared.

I wasn't positive because I had never heard my Sunday School teacher talk about this sort of stuff, but I was pretty sure that this was a sin. For a little Evangelical kid, I knew that it felt too good not to be a sin. All I could think about was what if I died that night? I'd surely go straight to Hell.

But those images couldn't escape my mind.

And those men...

Why could I not stop looking at them? Why did I not care about the women? I'm pretty sure I was supposed to look at them instead!

I was too confused. I didn't know what to think, and the fear didn't help.

I started tearing up, and praying really hard.

"God, I'm sorry. I'm really, really sorry," I muttered quietly between silent sobs. "I think that was wrong. Please forgive me, God. Please forgive me."

I finally prayed myself to sleep.

———————

A few weeks later, I finally had a name for what I experienced that night. It was a typical Sunday morning of the entire family fighting as we traveled to church, only to walk in the door with nothing but smiles and laughter. The little sanctuary was about half full, as usual, and our preacher began speaking.

He threw the Bible up in the air and waved it around as he bellowed about some place named Sodom. He was a good preacher, I have to admit. His voice echoed through the small country church as ladies fanned their faces from the hot summer heat. I sat in my normal place in the pew, beside my aunt, coloring on a book I got from Sunday school. I half-listened to what the preacher was saying.

"These men of Sodom wanted to take these visiting men out in to the street and have sexual relations with them. Imagine! Men wanting to have sex with other men!"

I looked up from the book I was tinkering with in the pew. He definitely had my attention now.

So, that does happen? I'm not alone!

My heart started racing as I relived that night from a few weeks ago.

"Let me tell you this, brothers and sisters: that is an abomination before God! It is unnatural and God hates it, because it goes against what he created! Homosexuals are the reason God destroyed Sodom and Gomorrah!"

Uh-oh, I thought, as I heard echoes of "Amen" around the small sanctuary.

He kept talking about these "homosexuals." That was a new word for me, but apparently that was what these men who wanted to have sex with other men were called. Later in the sermon, he had shortened it to "gay." That word was a little more familiar to me. I had heard some older people use that word before, but it was never in a positive light.

Is that what I am? Am I a "gay"?

Those same fears from that night on the Internet started creeping back. I squirmed in the pew.

If I were one of these "gays," did that mean that God hated me, too? Was he going to kill me with burning sulfur falling from the sky? I don't think I'm a gay.

I tried to zone out again into my coloring book, telling myself that I was not really one of those "gays."

This is probably a phase. Yeah…a phase.

———————————

But, the phase kept growing.

There is one thing you can never do as a child: you can never get back your innocence.

Once you know what sex is, it starts to invade your mind. Curiosity gets the best of you as your hormones begin rolling, and just about everything you see or hear or feel or think relates back to sex. For some people, it's like that for the rest of their lives. But when you're at that age, it's all brand new to you, and it's powerful. You're not quite sure what to do with it.

It was no different for me.

I couldn't even watch the Disney Channel anymore without one of the boys catching my eye.

But, I was also starting to become a little angry. All of the other boys at school were starting to discover sex, too, and they always talked about the girls. Really, that's all they talked about. Girls, girls, girls. It was aggravating.

"Look at her."

"Woah, I saw some women in my dad's magazine."

"She has big boobs!"

I just didn't get it, and that severely pissed me off, because I wanted so badly to "get it."

So, I went back to the internet to try and figure things out. This time, though, I tried reasoning with God.

"Okay, God, look. I know looking at this stuff is probably a sin. But, I have to! I know you don't like the gays, and I'm scared that if I don't make myself like women, I'll become one of them. So, I have to look at this stuff to make me like women. I promise, as soon as I begin to like women, I'll quit looking."

So, I tried.

And, boy, did I try hard.

I watched, and watched, and watched, and watched.

The entire time though, my eyes always went back to watching the guys. Sometimes, I would even get frustrated when a woman would get in the way. and then I would get mad at myself for getting frustrated about that. It became a never ending cycle of frustration and tension.

Confusion.

That pretty much sums up how I was feeling.

So confused.

On one hand, I had these teachings: I had to be pure, undefiled by the world, and without sin for God to really love me, and that meant being totally clean in thought and action. It also definitely meant not being "a gay."

But on the other hand, I had these feelings – these thoughts – that I couldn't help. I had these attractions which I was told were an abomination, but I simply had no control over them. I looked at some of the boys my age and just wanted to be close to them, but then I heard over my shoulder from preachers - my own preacher - that God hated the way I felt, and that I was probably doomed for an eternity of damnation because of it.

That is a lot for a ten year old to take in!

But, I had no choice. Life was coming fast, and there was no stopping it.

Religion became, for me, a sort of consistency. It was something that had structure and stability. It gave me goals and passions to shoot for in a world that was quickly changing and was confusing as hell for my pre-pubescent mind.

I embraced it harder than I ever had before.

I had to make God love me, because if I didn't, I was doomed.

I had no other choice because I was confused.

I was scared.

And I couldn't tell a soul.

Chapter Three

Being gay in the evangelical church is lonely; it's even more lonely when you're a pre-teen.

As I was approaching the teenage years, I was starting to realize that this was more than just a phase. But, I didn't want to acknowledge that just yet. The worst part, though, was the all-consuming fear that someone might find out the way I really felt, or what I was really thinking. I had heard how my friends and mentors talked about gay people, and I didn't want to be the butt of their jokes.

Even when others don't know how you are really feeling, you still feel like an outcast. When the other boys make their jokes, you just laugh along like you are the same way. You comment on girls just like they do, just so you'll fit in. Even though it all feels so alien to you, you give in because you don't want to stand out.

Around this same time, my dad bought a large piece of land in the Ozark Mountains in Arkansas. It was about two hours away from our home, and it was in the middle of nowhere. We had set up a deer camp, and began spending all of our weekends there. It was like a weekly family getaway, and other than having to wake up early to go deer hunting, it was actually pretty nice.

It was usually my mom, dad, and I, as well as my dad's sister and her husband. Sometimes, though, my older sister and her new husband would come. It was always more fun when they came, because there was actually someone closer to my age, even if it was by seven years. Occasionally, my older brother from Indiana would come down for a weekend and spend time with us. These were always my favorite weekends because I didn't get to see my older brother that often.

He graduated from high school as I entered Kindergarten, and then he moved to Indiana. He was my hero, as per usual with older brothers. He would call and talk to me every week or so, and always come down and bring me something from the city whenever he had a chance. When he would come to deer camp and stay with us, he and I would play games all weekend because there weren't all of the distractions of TV or the Internet. For my family and me, deer camp became a very special place. However, since we went every weekend, this meant that we dropped out of church almost completely.

I had become okay with this, though.

I wasn't happy that we weren't going anymore because of the church itself, by any means. I loved - and still love - the people at that church. It was the church that my dad grew up in, as well. My Sunday school teacher for all of those years is still someone I think of very fondly.

And it wasn't because I had lost faith, either.

On the contrary, I had more faith than ever before - but it was the kind of faith where I believed God was ready to strike me down at any minute. Frankly, I was tired of hearing about how much God was upset with me. I would leave every Sunday feeling more guilty than when I came in, because I could not stop these feelings toward other boys.

It was getting old.

So, not having to sit through that every Sunday was a little bit of relief.

———————

My birthday fell around the same time school let out for the summer. I was turning thirteen and was getting ready to go into the seventh grade, which was a big deal, because in our small town, seventh grade meant high school. I was ready for a change, too. That summer, for me, meant prospect, renovation, and new starts.

I was taking control of my own life.

Little did I know at the time, there are some things in life that you cannot change.

I was still watching straight porn to try and make myself attracted to women, but it just wasn't working. By this time I had a computer moved into my own bedroom, so it had become much easier, and my parents were still completely oblivious.

Summer had begun, which meant I could also stay up as late as I wanted.

One night at the outset of summer, my spirit of curiosity was getting the best of my pubescent mind. So far, this whole gay thing was just a theory. First of all, I wasn't even sure how "it" worked. Secondly, I wasn't even really sure that I was gay. I knew I enjoyed seeing those men naked, and that I thought boys my age were cute, but that's about all I knew.

I had been watching a few minutes of straight porn that night, but to no avail.

I knew I was wasting my time, and I had become utterly bored with the whole ritual.

I let my cursor slide over to the search box, and I began typing.

"G"

I took a deep breath.

Should I really do this? What if I like it?, I thought.

"Ga" I typed slowly.

Sweat started beading up on my forehead.

But maybe I won't like it? Maybe it will prove that I'm not gay, and that all of this was just a phase.

It sounded logical enough to me.

"Gay porn," I typed out, finally.

I took another deep breath, deliberated again for another second, and then pressed the return key.

In about a minute, the page finally loaded, full of pictures.

Woah.

My heart beat faster than it ever had before. My stomach turned inside out, knotted up, and then turned over. My palms were sweating. It was just too much. As I had feared, I was right all along. It wasn't just a phase, and this just proved it.

As my eyes gazed upon those pictures, all of the slight feelings I had felt before were now more intense than ever.

I liked it. A lot.

Too much, really.

So much that it scared me.

I hurried up and closed the browser and ran to the bathroom. I splashed cold water on my face to cool me down, but it wasn't really doing the trick. Everything I had experienced over the last few years suddenly made sense to me, and I didn't like the conclusion. All of the thoughts, the feelings, the attractions - all of it was now clear.

I'm gay.

I stared at myself in the mirror. My thirteen-year old, chubby, short-haired self looked into the reflection of my own eyes as the tears began to form and roll down my cheek. The words started to form in my mouth, but I wouldn't let them come out — I couldn't let them come out!

If I said it, then it would mean that it was true, and out of anything else in this world, I didn't want it to be true.

Another tear began to fall. I knew I had to say it. But I hated the words so badly in that moment that they were like fire upon my tongue.

This can't be true. Why does this have to be true?, I thought to myself.

Another tear fell down my cheek as I stared into the mirror.

I hated my reflection. I hated who I was. I hated everything about me.

Why would you do this God?

Everything was blurry. I despised my life. I despised God. I hated it all.

I don't understand. I don't get it. All I've done is try to make you happy.

I tried making some utterance of sound through my already whimpering lips.

"I'm…….gay." I finally whispered under my crying breath. The words did not taste as bad as I thought they would.

Surprisingly, there was some strength in finally getting that out in the air and hearing those words come from my own mouth.

I tried again, a little louder, but not loud enough that anyone could hear me.

"I'm…gay."

I wiped the tears away and sniffed.

One more time.

"I'm gay!"

This time, though, the newfound strength had turned a little angry.

"I'm gay!" I snarled at myself in the mirror.

I thought, *I'm gay? Are you kidding me?*

My anger began to boil.

God, I'm gay? Seriously?

I pulled my fist back to punch the mirror, but I knew that would wake my parents, which would lead to questions. And I sure as hell didn't want questions right now.

All I had were questions. I wanted answers. Answers that I was not getting. Answers to questions I didn't even know how to ask.

Without the outlet of punching something, I simply fell to the floor, threw my head in my arms, and sobbed.

I sat there and wept in the bathroom floor for Lord knows how long.

I just cried and prayed.

I asked God a billion times that night to just take it away.

Can't you change this, God? Can't you make me like girls like everyone else?

I didn't need this. I didn't want this. I just wanted to be a regular kid.

I wanted to be a normal straight guy, who grows up and goes to college, then finds a woman, gets married, has some kids, works, goes to church, dies, and then goes to Heaven.

I just wanted to be normal. I just wanted to be like everyone else. Why is that too much to ask, God?

My head started swimming as I curled in the floor and cried.

God, if you hate gay people, does that mean you hate me, too? All I've done is try to please you. Is that not enough? I don't want this! Does that count for some-

thing? Since I can't help the way I feel, does this mean you made me this way? But, if you made me this way, and gay people go to Hell, does that mean you created me for Hell?

The loneliness was growing intense. Not only did I feel like an outcast to all of the other people my age, now I was feeling like I was an outcast to God.

I felt completely and utterly alone.

The Bible says you love me, though, God. So, there's no way you could have created me just so you could torture me. That just doesn't sound right.

My questions kept compiling.

Maybe I can fix this? Maybe if I work hard enough and pray hard enough, this will go away? God, if I'm good enough, will you get rid of this for me? Please?

I didn't get an answer. But, nonetheless, I still made up my mind that I was supposed to be straight, and by God, I was going to be. I was going to be the best Christian the world had ever seen, and God was going to change it for me then. It was just going to take time, energy, and a lot of prayer. But, surely, God wouldn't abandon me on this. Because God hated gays, right? Surely he would fix this for me since I didn't want to be one of them.

There is one thing ex-gay ministries don't tell you in their brochures: it's not possible to pray the gay away.

Well, at least that's the consensus I get from people I know who have been through some of those ministries. Even though I never went through one myself, I can still attest to this from my own experience.

If there were ever any case in which praying the gay away should have worked, it would have been with me. I promise you, I have to be on the list of the top ten people who have prayed that prayer. It was my mantra.

I took the verse "Pray without ceasing" quite seriously. Often times, it was like a skipping record as I prayed over it in every spare moment that I had.

I had a system down.

Every time I prayed, I included it in the prayer somewhere. It would be something like, "God, please take away this thorn in my flesh that is homosexuality." Yes, I really used to pray like that as an early teen. I was a good Baptist boy.

Whenever I slipped up and had a gay thought, I would instantly repent. I would say, "God, please forgive me for feeling that way, or for having those lustful thoughts."

I would fast every once in a while, just to prove to God how important it was to me. Sometimes, I would fast from food. Other times, I would fast from television, or the Internet, or something else I enjoyed. The last part of my system was the most important: I would always end the day with some sort of mega-prayer, begging God's forgiveness for having these feelings, and asking Him to take it away.

I had become a monk in my own right with these prayers. I remember one night I even prayed to God that if I ever slipped up and decided to act on my feelings, that he just kill me before I could do it.

This lasted for the first part of my high school career. I made it through both seventh and eighth grade with this mindset.

I gave it everything I had, but my hormones just couldn't handle it anymore. I couldn't quit thinking about boys!

By the time I was fifteen, it had become a constant thing.

It didn't help that I played football and had to share a locker room with a lot of these guys.

Wow, he's cute. Look at that hair. No, stop that, Brandon. That's not Godly. But, he's muscular, too. And those eyes! Quit it, Brandon, you're going to go to Hell thinking like that. Oh, he smiled! Look at that smile. It makes me all giddy. Brandon, stop it! Now pray! God, forgive me for my lustful thoughts. I repent. Woah, he just took his shirt off. Damn it, Brandon! I repent, I repent, I repent!

It was a lost cause. I had given it everything I had for two years, and nothing was working. If anything, it was getting worse. I finally conceded that God wasn't going to take this away from me.

But, this left me in quite the predicament, for a number of reasons. One, I believed God hated gay people. I had that one down pat, and there was no wavering or room for discussion. It was in the Bible, plain as day, and as far as my fifteen-year-old mind was concerned, the debate was over. Two, I now knew that my feelings were not going to change. I knew that I wanted to be with another boy and had no concern whatsoever with being with a girl. There was not even a curiosity. I knew what I wanted, unfortunately. Now, most people at this point would just say, "Okay, well if that's the way it is and I'm going to Hell anyway, I might as well just enjoy life as I know it and try to hurry this process up. Bring on the boys!"

But, I couldn't. My faith and spirituality were too big of a part of my life. Also, I still had a deep feeling that God wanted to use me for ministry of some kind. That hadn't gone away. It was always there, just like my attraction to guys. So, how was I to merge all of these things? This began to conquer my thought life and led to multiple sleepless nights.

How was I going to converge a God that doesn't like gay people, with accepting me, a gay boy, who wants to be in the ministry?

After mulling it over, I finally had an answer.

I knew I couldn't get God to like me, the real Brandon. So, I set out on a mission to create a fake-Brandon. This fake-Brandon would be the Brandon I presented to the world. I hoped that not only could I make the world like him, I could make God like him, too. Enough so that when I died, he would let me in to Heaven for all the good things that fake-Brandon did.

Again, it made sense to me.

Thus began what I called "The Game."

———————————

The Game is what I played, and I was good at it, too. The Game began when Straight-Face came on the scene. Straight-Face was my personal mask. The point of the Game was to make people believe that Straight-Face was the real-Brandon. I had to get them to like Straight-Face, and not see that the boy wearing the mask was scared, hurt, and confused. Instead, they needed to see nothing but spirituality, goodness, masculinity, and assertiveness.

Straight-Face was everything I wanted to be, and portrayed all of the characteristics I wanted to be true about myself.

The Game was a game of deception. It relied on the theory that if you tell a lie long enough, it becomes true.

And oh, how badly I wanted it to be true.

Mainly, I just wanted to be free. I wanted to be anything other than what I was.

I knew that for this plan to work, I had to get into a church again. I had to dive in and attack Hell with a water pistol so that, hopefully, I would finally get some recognition from God, even if I had to hide behind a mask to get it.

So, that's what I did.

The buzzer had buzzed; The Game had commenced.

Now, I'm not saying people didn't know me at all while I was playing the Game. Straight-Face still had parts of me. But only the parts

I wanted people to see, and those I magnified. I really did have a strong spiritual side, and I really did believe most of what I was saying at the time. But Straight-Face would only let the world see the times when I had it all together. Never could they see the pain, the doubts, and the struggles. I really was assertive, in a sense. But Straight-Face only showed others the accomplishments, never the failures that were happening every day.

———————————

The Baptist church in my town had a fairly good sized youth ministry for a small town. I had heard the youth minister there was a really funny guy, so I thought I would give it a shot. I convinced my dad to take me to church there one Sunday night, and it just so happened that after the service that night, the youth were going out for pizza. They invited me along, so I went.

I was pretty new at the Game at this point, so I didn't have everything down just yet. Luckily, I had already had some experience at acting, because I had spent the last five years hiding the fact that I was attracted to boys. However, I wasn't that good at it yet. So, it made for some awkward moments.

It had been a while since I was around "church people," and even when I was around church people, it was rarely people my own age. At the small church we used to go to, it was mostly people forty and older. The people I hung out with at school weren't really church people, either. But I ad-libbed the best that I could. Straight-Face was on, and we were ready to try this out.

The youth group of about twenty kids all sat around the long table at Pizza Hut, waiting for our pizza's to arrive. It was your normal, rowdy youth group, with students ranging from seventh to twelfth grade.

I guess since I was the new guy, the youth minister stayed close to me. He sat across from me, and tried to keep conversation going. I could tell the guy genuinely cared for me, and for the other students. I liked the guy already.

"So, have you been in church much, Brandon?" he asked.

"Yeah, I mean, our family used to go to church every Sunday when I was younger."

"Oh, yeah? Why'd you stop?"

"Well, my dad got a job and he has to kind of go out of town every weekend just to get a break from his work. So we started going out of town, and kind of quit going to church."

Well, that wasn't a very good answer. This guy needs to know I'm spiritual. I can't let him think I'm a heathen!

"But I still stay pretty involved in the faith," I continued, "I still pray a lot, and read about a bunch of crap online."

Did I just say crap? That's not good language for church people. Oh, no!

"Excuse my language." I said, embarrassed.

"Don't you ever use that kind of language around me again," he said.

He said it so stone-faced. I know my face was as red as the pepperoni on my pizza.

Then he laughed.

Joking.

He was joking! Whew.

I had side-stepped that one. I laughed along, but I realized the Game was going to be harder than I thought. But I was in it for the long haul. Straight-Face was on for good, and I was not going to let my attractions keep me from becoming the person I was supposed to be. This was my Game, and I was going to win.

_____

One of the main marks of the modern American church is that it encourages us to create these pseudo-realities for ourselves. I didn't realize it at the time, but I know now, that we all have our own masks. It's who we are when we step through those church doors, or when we're around other Christians. We have to "live up" to what we're expected to be, so we end up working so hard to be that person, even though the person we really are is so far away from who the mask pretends to be. I have my Straight-Face, but others have Sober-Face, or Not-Depressed-Face, or Fill-In-The-Blank-Face.

The problem with masks, though, is that eventually they start suffocating you.

On top of that, you become dependent on the mask for your faith to work. One day you wake up and realize that your faith has been stolen by the mask. When the mask comes off, so does your faith. I began to notice this pattern in my own life.

Straight-Face would come alive when I awoke in the morning and sprinted off to school, usually carrying a Bible in my backpack. He was there through the Fellowship of Christian Athletes meetings before the first class. He was in charge while I sat through my classes, being the good student that I was expected to be. He was the one called on during football games to lead the team prayer. He was there while hanging out with church friends after school. He was on while I was hanging out with my family at the house, and he was definitely on when I read my Bible at night and said my prayers.

However, once everyone was asleep, and I had already done my nightly routine of Bible-reading and prayer, Straight-Face finally came off.

For a little while — even if it were only a half hour a night — I was able to be me without having to pretend to be someone else. That little bit of time every night, tucked quietly in my bedroom in the back corner of the small, country house, was the only time I was able to not wear my mask. When I first started the Game, I felt guilty for taking Straight-Face off at all. But, a person can only pretend for so long without going insane. Living in the closet is much like method acting. You entrench yourself in the role so deeply that you start to lose touch with reality. A few weeks after I started the Game, I found myself letting my guard down at night, once I was alone. I tried to keep myself in the role, but I realized pretty quickly it was useless. No matter how hard you try to suppress the real you, it is not going to be silenced. The rest of the world may not be able to hear the real you screaming from behind the mask, but to the person behind the mask, it is deafening. I soon realized that I had to give myself some time every day to be me, and not to be so neurotic about wearing Straight-Face all of the time.

Besides, I thought, *everyone's asleep and I am alone.* I am safe when I am alone.

Honestly, I didn't like Straight-Face from the outset. He got on my nerves often. I guess I had already became envious of him. I know it sounds weird to be envious of an alter ego that you had created, but everyone loved Straight-Face. He was president of the class, leader of the clubs, and a mascot for the youth group. I envied the love he was getting. Now, I know that love was supposed to be projected towards me, but it never felt that way. I knew deep down that the person all of these people loved was Straight-Face, and not me.

I figured since that was true for people, it was probably true for God, as well. I figured he loved Straight-Face, but was pretty disgusted at the real-Brandon. Straight-Face was the perfect picture of the evangelical Christian student; the real-Brandon was a scared faggot who didn't really have a place in this world.

So, whenever the mask came off, sadly, my faith usually went with him.

Why not? God loved him, I thought, *not me.*

Chapter Four

Since Straight-Face was the one with the faith, once he was off late at night, I stopped caring.

Well, I tried anyway. A large part of me still cared, but I didn't want to care. It seemed pointless.

Before too long, I fell right back into the pit of the Internet, but this time I skipped all of the facades of trying to fake it. I relished the few hours a day where Straight-Face wasn't controlling my life and bottling up all of my feelings and attractions.

This isn't to say that the real me didn't feel guilty about what I was doing. I still felt like it was wrong, and that God hated what I was doing, but I just didn't care.

I had tried to change. I gave it my all, but nothing worked.

If God didn't care enough to change me after I had tried so hard, why should I? I would just let Straight-Face handle the faith stuff, and in my few short hours a week as the real me, I would do what I wanted.

We were becoming total opposites. He was succeeding more and more; I was falling further and further. The happier he appeared to be, the more depressed I was becoming.

I was now in my junior year of high school, and Straight-Face was making the bold move to answer the call to ministry. It was a quick, public ceremony, in which you stood before the congregation and your pastor announces that you are committing to living a life of ministry. I smiled shyly as I stood next to my youth minister, looking out upon the congregation.

Boy, did Straight-Face have everyone fooled! I stood here in front of them as the perfect example of a good, Evangelical Christian boy. I didn't drink. I didn't smoke. I didn't cuss. And I didn't date girls that did.

Well, I didn't date any girls, actually. There was not even a part of me that wanted to attempt it. I went on a few dates sporadically, but I could count them all on one hand. The few times I did go out, it was awkward. It wasn't the girls' fault in any way - I just didn't care to be there. We would hold hands, and all I could do was wish that it was the hand of the boy I was crushing on at the time. Then, because I couldn't control the thoughts, I would get angry with myself and feel defeated.

Why can't you just enjoy this?, Straight-Face would ask in my ear, the scowling plea making my hands even clammier than they already were.

The dates always ended the same way. But, I do admit, I enjoyed the companionship during the few dates I had. It was really all I was looking for, or craving. I had created a world for myself that was nothing but loneliness. I felt like no one knew me, and if anyone did, that person wouldn't want to be around me. My family, my friends, even my God, were all in love with a fake person I had created, and so I was left hanging out to dry.

I resorted to what I knew to get rid of this feeling - the underside of the Internet. I tried hard to fight the temptation. Sometimes I would go weeks - even months - without ever giving into it, but ultimately the lack of intimacy would get the best of me, and I would seek it out.

I understand why people are so easily pulled into an addiction to pornography, because it is very deceptive. It catches you when you're at a low, promising to give you a sense of intimacy that you yearn for so badly. Sometimes, when you're at your lowest, you don't realize or even care if it's a false sense of intimacy because you just need something to help you feel alive. It pulls you in, promising to satisfy the intimate cravings that you have, but it leaves you only craving more. It doesn't really fulfill the one thing you're looking to get out of it.

Straight-Face and I stand before the congregation, peering out at the unsurprised, yet pleased, crowd of people. He smiles and nods graciously at the crowd, while inside I hunker down, guilt-ridden. The pastor closes out the service as the crowd applauds my decision, and I make my way to the fellowship hall of the church, where all of my friends have gathered together.

I notice two of my friends, a boy and a girl, were awfully close. I had suspected this would happen, and then I notice their hands are clasped. My chest, just seconds ago filled with excitement and joy, is now deflated. It wasn't because I particularly cared that these two were together. I had a crush on neither one of them. But, it was just a stark reminder at how different I was from the rest of my friends.

At sixteen, all of my friends were searching, dating, texting, and exploring their relationships. They seemed free in their exploits, and they seemed to be natural at it. Yet, here I was at the same age, just trying to do whatever I could to make God love me. I didn't have time to act like a teenager; I was too busy trying to make myself straight. It was sort of paradoxical, as well. I envied my friends because they were getting to do normal teenager things, but at the same time, I took pride in the fact that I didn't. It would not sit well with my trying to bribe God to love me for me to go out and act this way.

I didn't realize it then, but now I know that I was not that different from many conservative Christians in this respect. Many Christians have one thing in their focus: getting to Heaven. The decisions they make, the things they stand for and stand against, and the words they wisely (and sometimes, unwisely) choose all revolve around a fear of going to Hell. They, too, are wearing their masks, trying so hard to make God love them. But, there is a bit of pride that comes with this, too.

Pride may not be the most appropriate word to use. It's more like pride mixed with reassurance. You have to feel like you've done something in order to assure yourself that you are in good standing with God. It comes with the territory of believing in a God that requires masks. You see, mask-wearing is at the heart of Evangelical Christianity. The belief is that God's love really is conditional. It only comes after you have been "covered" by the blood of Christ. If you are not hiding behind the mask of Christ's blood, then God is ready to strike you down because of your sin. Evangelicals constantly wear masks to try and cover who they really are, both from God and from other people.

This is the same pride that Straight-Face fed upon. Straight-Face didn't go out and party, or sleep around, or even talk back to teachers at school, because Straight-Face had to prove to everyone else that he was different, set-apart, and actually saved. But really, I think the only one I was trying to convince was myself. At the end of the day, I was the one that needed the reassurance just so I could sleep at night. I couldn't live with the thought of God's hating me and always being ready to destroy me, so I needed those little daily reminders that I was in good standing with God.

It came with a cost, though, and that cost was staring at me as I saw my friends clasp their hands together. I wanted that. I needed that. I just wanted to know what it felt like to be with someone that I wanted to be with, and they wanted to be with me. To feel that connection, that intimacy.

I think one of the biggest misconceptions in the conservative world is that being gay is all about sex. But in reality, it's not at all. Sure, there are some in the gay world who idolize sex, but you have that in the straight world just as much. Even as a sixteen year old, it was about something much deeper than sex.

It's all about chemistry. It's about connecting with another person on a level that words cannot even describe. Every romantic comedy, television show, or story made me feel as if I was missing out on the one thing that connects all of humanity. When you deny yourself — or you are denied by others — the freedom to express yourself in love, it creates an inner turmoil that is sometimes too much to cope with — especially as a teenager.

This is also why one can't fake it and try to be with someone he or she has no connection with. If there is no chemistry between the two, the intimacy is lost. To be blunt, I could physically be with a girl, but it would just be an action. It would be the same as if a straight person tried to physically be with someone of the same gender. While it's possible, it doesn't mean there would be chemistry, or even any enjoyment. I have tried to force it and make myself love a girl, but it just doesn't work. A relationship without chemistry, like porn, leaves you more lonely than before, and really is unfulfilling at the end of the day. That is where I was at this point in my life.

I was just yearning for someone to connect with. I wanted someone to hold hands with and someone to cuddle. I knew after just a few dates with girls that that route was not going to work. So, I just left relationships, in general, well enough alone. But moments like these, when I saw my friends getting to explore this unknown territory, it made my heart crumble a little more.

This caused my loneliness to grow much deeper, and I was going a little crazy. I was a sixteen year old kid, full of angst, and feeling completely alone in this world. That was not a good combination. Soon, all of that trepidation began to bubble over.

———————

It seemed like the more people began to love Straight-Face, the more I hated myself. The pressure was building, and I was about to burst. I didn't think I could live up to the pedestal that people were putting Straight-Face on. I felt like, eventually, I was going to let everyone down – my parents and God included – whenever the real me was exposed, and I didn't know if I wanted that to happen. Ever.

I had had some suicidal thoughts before, especially around age thirteen when I first made the cognitive recognition that I was gay.

But, this time it was different. Before, it was just passing thoughts; but, now I was starting to think about it on a much deeper level. I would sometimes daydream about it. I would be driving my car, just wishing my tire would blow out and run me into a big truck, ending it all in one quick smash.

The more the pressure built up inside me, the more I didn't think I could live that way anymore.

I mean, it's hard enough just being yourself, especially as a teenager. But, when you have to be yourself and somebody else, it's too much to deal with. You can't do it.

Finally, I had had enough.

It had just been a few weeks since I stood before my congregation and told them I was committing to a life of ministry. My parents were out of town for the weekend, like most weekends, but now that I was driving on my own, I had the option of staying at home. I chose to stay home quite often. One reason was because I didn't really care to spend my weekends in the Ozark Mountains anymore, and second, Straight-Face didn't want to miss church on Sundays.

Usually, I would have a friend or two over and we'd hang out all weekend, just goofing off, playing video games, and watching movies. But this particular weekend, I was by myself, and that did not help the depression and loneliness that had been building. I finally had decided I was tired of playing this game with God, with my friends, with my family, with myself, and with life. It would be easier just to be dead. I had hit the darkest of the darkness.

God, I know this is probably not going to get me into Heaven, but I don't know what else to do. I might as well take my chances, because it looks like I'm not going to get into Heaven anyway. I can't handle this. I can't beat this. I hate being fake. But if I'm honest with everyone, I'll be hated. It's not fair. I just don't want to live anymore. Why did you ever make me in the first place?

But God wasn't answering me, and that just fueled the fire. I went into my parent's bedroom and opened the gun safe. I pulled out the 20-gauge Remington shotgun and held it in my hands as tears welled up in my eyes.

I remember the cold steel of the gun in my hands as I pulled it out of the black safe. I stared at it for a good while.

Is this what you want, God? Do I just need to do us both a favor and do this? Why won't you answer me?!

I reached around the top of the safe until I found a bullet, and I loaded it into the gun.

God, I don't know what else to do. I just don't know what else to do.

I kept repeating that line in my head, and sometimes out loud.

Everything happened in what seemed like two minutes but also five hours. I know not much time had passed, but every second felt like a year.

I took the gun to my bedroom and I sat on my bed. I studied the gun in my hands, wondering how things had come to this, and what people were going to think when Brandon, the kid who "had it all together and was the happiest boy in school," shot himself?

I just don't know what else to do.

I wondered why God ever made me in the first place. Why would he put this on someone? Why would he allow this to happen to me, when all I've ever done is try to make him happy? I had always heard my Bible teachers say that everyone was a beautiful creation, made in his image, but it never seemed to apply to me. It sure didn't feel like it when all I ever heard from these same people is that gay people were horrible and deserving of being burned for an endless eternity. I sure didn't feel like I had done anything to be deserving of eternal hell fire, but I sure believed it because that's all I had ever been taught.

The more I thought on these things, the more my sadness started turning into anger. Suddenly, it became less about my pain, and more about being angry at everyone and everything: angry with God, angry with family, angry with friends, and angry with the way society hated gay people so much.

Maybe if I do this, it will make a statement. Maybe they will hurt like I hurt.

My mind raced, thinking about all of the ways I was hurting.

I kept studying the gun.

Without even thinking about it, I loaded the bullet into the chamber. The *click-clack* of the gun loading the bullet sent shivers down my spine as I wiped away more tears from my cheek.

My heart was beating so fast I thought it was going to burst through my chest. I thought about my parents. It would not be fair for them to come home and see this. They didn't deserve that. I should at least go out into the woods and do it. Not here, though. This is their home. Every time they come home from this point forward, all they will be able to see is the blood stains they first saw when they walked into my bedroom. All they will ever be able to see again is what remains of their baby boy.

It occurred to me that I hadn't taken a breath in more than a minute, and I gasped loudly for air. Like a tsunami wave hitting a stunned crowd, I suddenly had the realization of how real this was becoming. I really didn't want to kill myself, but I didn't want to be alive, either. If I did this, I would at least be able to escape my mask — but for what gain?

Just do it and get it over with, I told myself.

I was fighting with my own mind, trying to decide what to do.

If I do this, how will my family react? I don't think mom and dad could ever get over this. You don't want to do that to them.

Clarity and reasoning were trying to seep their way back into my consciousness.

They don't understand the pain, though. I don't know how I'm going to live my whole life in this fake reality. I can't do this much longer.

The scales were teetering back and forth, and I wasn't sure which side was going to win.

Straight-Face was trying to remind me of how this would seal our fate for good.

There is no way you're going to Heaven if you do this, he said. *No way! You have to keep fighting; keep pushing through.*

In moments like this, though, theology is the last thing you want to think about. All you can ask yourself is "Where is God, and why should I care?" I had pled with God until I was blue in the face, but he hadn't changed anything yet.

I laid back on my bed, gun still there with me, and continued praying, arguing with myself and with God. I started dozing off as I continued battling it out in my mind, so I laid the gun down beside my bed. All I felt inside was that I was tired of being alive, but now I felt worse because I felt like I was too much of a coward to do anything about it. With all of the jumbled thoughts scrambling in my mind, I finally drifted off to sleep.

AGHHHHHHHHHH!

The alarm clock blared in my ear like a car coming to a crash, and I shot up out of bed, exhilarated. I stared at the gun beside the bed, and I physically shook at the thought that I almost didn't make it through the night.

It was almost like a moment of sobriety. I couldn't believe that it almost happened, and I knew I couldn't let it happen again because I didn't know if next time I would be able to talk myself out of it or not. I jumped up out of bed, put the gun safely away so that my parents wouldn't question anything, and got ready for church.

Church was home for Straight-Face. He shined on Sunday mornings. He was always dressed nicely, wearing a smile and walking into the building like he owned the place. Old ladies loved him; old men wanted to shake his hand. Straight-Face knew how to play the religious crowd, and he was damn good at it, too. He always balanced out the good belly laugh with the twinkle of the "I'm praying for you." This was his domain.

All the while, I was trapped inside, watching him masquerade.

Not that the words coming out of my mouth were not completely genuine. I believed there was a God. I believed in prayer. I legitimately liked (some of) these folks. But Straight-Face always took it to the next level. I was really beginning to hate him more and more, but I didn't know how to stop him.

Plus, I had to have him.

I loved God because I had to do so in order to stay out of Hell, and honestly I loved being a part of the religious life. But, I couldn't continue in my religion and be who I truly was. I needed Straight-Face so that I could go to church and feel like I was accepted there. It was a catch-22 that was driving me insane; but, it didn't do any good to complain. As much as I hated that mask, I was stuck.

I was held captive by my own invention.

Straight-Face had good friends there, too. It was nice having a place to go to, week after week, where most of the faces stayed the same, and it remained stable.

It was here at this little country Baptist church that I began to learn about community and how important it is in life. It wasn't that they were the shining example of community by any stretch of the imagination. In fact, the reason I learned the importance of community is because even while I was at church, I felt totally alone. I craved having others to share life with in a real way, and not just in passing. I had seen on television and read online about other gay people who were open and out, and people still loved them. I wanted that.

I knew I wouldn't have that here in my small Arkansas town, though. I was beginning to long for someone to know the real me, but I just couldn't tell anyone.

When you're in a conservative Evangelical church and you are gay, you can't come out of the closet. It's like an unwritten rule. As soon as you do, you're an outcast. Now, they may claim that you won't be an outcast, but you know you will be. You can feel it, because you know the way they work. You have been a part of their world, and sitting in the closet, you have heard the way they talk about gay people. You don't want to be just another piece of gossip for them.

"Have you heard so-and-so is gay? Such a shame. Poor soul."

"I wouldn't let him around my family, I tell you what."

"I hear so-and-so is a lesbian. She is just looking for attention, I think."

Even though you know a lot of them won't publicly attack you, you know that if they knew about you, things would be completely different. They wouldn't want to hang around you anymore, or be seen with you again. Once you have gay cooties, I think everybody is afraid they will catch the cooties and suddenly become gay.

So you bottle it up, and you leave it inside to stew some more. You join in the jokes with them, never letting on that every time you hear it, the pressure builds a little more. You are stuck within the shell of the mask with nowhere to turn.

This is why I was aching for community.

I wanted to release that pressure that was building. I wanted to just tell someone - anyone - who I really was. For years, nobody ever really knew me. They knew parts of me. But, nobody really knew me. I wanted someone to know me, and then to hug me, and tell me they loved me anyway.

Not everyone has this experience, I know. Some people who grew up gay in the Evangelical church just embraced their homosexual feelings, and really didn't care to be thrown out.

But, I couldn't afford that. I had already bought in to their theology - hook, line, and sinker. Plus, I felt I was supposed to be in the ministry. So, I didn't really have a choice. I couldn't tell anyone – even my closest friends – because if they cracked under pressure, or got mad at me and told others, then my entire future plans would go out the window. There was just simply nothing I could do about the situation. I was caught between two places, and I couldn't change it.

I made it work, though. The other side of the story is that I truly did believe the theology that they were teaching me. I was now seventeen at this point, and I had never actually acted upon my attractions, even though I wanted to so badly. On top of that, I had really fought hard against succumbing to the dark side of the Internet. I was feeling like even though I hadn't been able to change my attractions, I had at least gotten them under control to the point that God must have loved Straight-Face, which meant he probably loved me, too. I crossed my fingers anyway.

So, I just went on with life, pushing the rainbow parts of me to the back, trying to ignore it and act like it wasn't there. My attractions, however, would remind me often that they were there. Usually when I passed swimming pools filled with a bunch of shirtless guys my age. When you're in the closet, you begin to both love and hate swimming pools.

Chapter Five

"Allan is going through a really hard time right now," my mom said.

I could tell she was beating around the bush. I had a knack for picking up on my mom's emotions.

I knew I had to press the issue. I mean, we were talking about my older brother — my hero! If something was going on with him, I needed to know. My thoughts began to reflect back on my relationship with him.

I remember standing in my tuxedo on his wedding day when I was about twelve years old. I had to have been the youngest groomsman ever, and the old ladies seemed to dig that.

I watched him say his vows, and I watched him get the garter off of his bride with his teeth. I think I commented on how disgusting and weird that was, to which my mom told me to be quiet, apologizing to the table guests.

I was there when his son was born. It was my second time being an uncle, and it was always a cool experience because, well, I was just a young teenager. I liked having the title "Uncle Brandon." It had a nice ring to it, I thought.

I was also there when he and his wife split suddenly for some reason that no one really knew. They were both claiming some pretty big things, even though no one would give me a clear story.

Since I was fifteen at the time, my dad let me go stay a week with him in Indiana a few weeks after he and his wife split. We bonded more that week than we ever have, because now that I was older, we were finally relating on the same level.

We also really bonded because of how he acted - even though I don't think he had a clue as to what I was picking up.

He had a friend who was staying with him in his new apartment. I watched these two interact, and all I could think was, "I want a friend like that!"

They would lie beside each other on the floor and watch television. They would sit across from each other at restaurants, and constantly make jokes and giggle and laugh. It was unlike any friendship I had, but it was exactly the kind of friendship I was craving because it seemed like more than a friendship. When they were together, they acted more like kids than I did. My brother was happier with his new friend than I had ever seen him with his ex-wife.

After I left, I began to suspect things about that friendship, even though I brushed it off.

Now that I was eighteen, I had enough time to process all that happened that week, and I had a gut feeling about where this conversation was going.

"Why is he having a hard time?" I finally replied back to my mom.

"Well, it's just that he and your dad aren't exactly getting along."

"Why not?" I continued.

Since I learned how to talk, I have always been good at "the question game." I think I was destined for a philosophy degree from birth because I always prodded and asked questions until I got an answer.

And I knew my mom always cracked eventually.

"Just because of the way Allan is living right now. He and your dad just don't really agree on it," my mom stammered to reply. She was trying to brush off my questions, but I wouldn't relent.

"How is he living?"

"Just…it's….I don't know. Just don't talk to your dad about it, okay!"

She was cracking. This didn't take long.

"Well, it has to be something."

"Yeah, it's something. It's…complicated."

"Mom?"

"What?" she shot back, exasperated. She always hated when I made her crack.

"Is Allan gay?"

I think she was more relieved than I was. At least this way, she didn't actually tell me. She just nodded her head.

I knew it! This is…this is…this is huge!

"That's disgusting!" said Straight-Face, snarling his upper lip and nose. I couldn't let on that my mind was racing.

For so long, I shrugged off those thoughts about my brother, but now they were confirmed.

I used to get so pissed because I was the gay brother. But now, I finally find out that he is gay, too. I just wanted to call him up on the phone and say, "Hey, bro, me too!"

I had so many questions. So many things I just wanted to say to him.

I wondered if he felt alone, too. I wondered what made him want to tell people. He was a Christian, as well. I wondered how he got past feeling like God hated him, or if he did get past it. I wondered if he had a Straight-Face as well, and I wondered how he finally took it off. So many questions!

"Well, just don't talk about it with your dad, please. He is not taking it very well," she added.

That was an understatement. My dad, who was raised strictly conservative Baptist, just couldn't come to terms with my brother's being gay and reconciling it with everything he was taught. He had a deep conviction that it was wrong. Every conversation they had over the phone ended up in an argument, with both hanging up in tears.

I felt sorry for my brother. But, at the same time, I felt sorry for my dad, too.

I saw how bad this was hurting him. I didn't really understand why it was hurting him, but I could see that it was.

He was becoming somewhat of a recluse, and my brother was a subject that only my mom and I talked about. Dad and I never talked about my brother. We tried a couple of times while playing golf, but it always ended with dad tearing up, and so I would quickly change the subject.

I hated seeing my dad this way.

As much as I had admired my brother for taking off his mask, and even though he was my hero, I was also angry at him.

Why was he doing this to Dad? I understand that he has these feelings, too, and can't help them. But, he should do like me and not tell anyone. Plus, didn't he realize God hated gay people? This was not good for him - or for his soul!

Thus, Straight-Face began to take over the situation. He knew what he had to do as a good, Evangelical Christian boy: he had to confront my brother about his sin.

———————————

I must have sounded like the biggest jerk on the planet in that e-mail.

I started by telling my brother that I loved him, and that I wasn't condemning him. I told him that I understood how much sin hurts and controls our life. I tried to explain to him that I knew how he felt, without letting on that I knew *exactly* how he felt. I talked in code, hoping that he wouldn't break my code.

Then I started in on the verses of Scripture that condemned homosexuality. I quoted every single one of them with astute clarity, pointing out the error of his ways. I likened his life to that of alcoholics and drug-addicts. I told him that his homosexual feelings were the work of Satan, and that it was most likely a demon controlling his life. I gave him steps, each with scriptural backing, of how to exorcise this demon from his life.

Sheesh. What a hypocrite I am, I thought as I typed away at my computer. *I'm giving him advice that's about as clear as I can make it, and yet, I can't even get this advice to work for me.*

Not that I didn't believe what I saying. I believed every word of it. It was all that I knew, all I was taught.

I sent the message, feeling like I probably made God pretty happy with that one. Straight-Face had done his Christian duty for the day, and hopefully, my brother's eyes would be opened and he would reject his homosexual feelings just like I was rejecting mine.

Only I wasn't *really* rejecting my feelings.

Because, well, that's impossible. You can't reject the way you feel. You can't change the way you feel. You just feel it.

Attraction is attraction, and you have no control over it.

I knew this all too well.

But when God is some being in the sky who is simply there to judge you, you become a little illogical. You begin to reason with God and yourself, weighing action against action.

True, I let my eyes wander sometimes, but it's not like what my brother is doing. He is accepting his feelings, and actually acting on them. That's really wrong. What I'm doing is just a little wrong.

Surprisingly, I got a response back from my brother pretty quickly. I read each word carefully, eating the words up. I was finally getting some sort of insight into my older brother's life. I was seeing past the veil of my hero and getting a glimpse into his true self. He described himself, his past, and where he was. He talked about Biblical interpretations and gave me other verses that countered mine.

Wow, he's done his homework.

The e-mail was long, and it took me a while to study it. However, I wouldn't let myself study it too much.

I was scared that it was possible that what he was saying was true, and I didn't want it to be true.

Conservative Christianity was all that I knew. It was my life. It was where I found my identity. If that were gone, who would I be? Plus, if it were true, I would be tempted to act on my feelings, and I just did not want to be known as a gay man.

So, even though I dove into that message, I simply replied back to him that I was praying for him and that I was there for him if he ever wanted to talk more in the future.

Those words, though.

Those words stuck with me. His view of God was so different from mine. It intrigued me.

At the end of the day, I knew I had too much to lose to listen to him. I chalked it up to his being deceived by the Devil, and moved on.

Besides, I was starting college soon, and I had done what I was supposed to do.

I got my points with God. I was set.

But, those words.

Chapter Six

My mom and dad gave me a hug as I put the final box in my dorm room. I could tell they were holding back their tears. I was their baby, their youngest, and I had officially moved into my freshman year of college. We all knew this was an entirely new season of our lives. We said our goodbyes, and they went back home. Luckily, the college I chose was only about an hour away from home. There were a couple of reasons for this. For one, I have always been close to my family, and I didn't want to be far from them. But, mostly, I was scared. I knew that if I moved away to be with entirely new people, in an entirely new place, that I would be tempted to be authentic about who I really was. I was scared of the temptation to come out. I had been taught to "flee from sexual immorality" in any way possible. For me, this meant making sure I was still around people that knew who I was - or really, knew who Straight-Face was - to keep myself from being tempted.

Starting college was an exciting time for me, though, as it is for any student. I was viewing college as a chance for renewal, growth, and starting over. Living in the closet in the Evangelical world really is just one long series of "starting over." Even though attraction is not something that you can change, you tell yourself daily that this time, it's going to work. True, I had long since given up on trying to change my attractions, but I was still daily battling my eyes and my wandering mind. I always looked for new benchmarks to say "from this point on, things are going to be different!" Starting college was one of those benchmarks.

The prospect of the change that was going to occur during college made me starry-eyed. I had already spoken with the Baptist Collegiate Ministry (BCM) there, and I was pumped about finally getting a start in ministry. I had big plans, and I was ready to take on the world!

I chatted with my new roommate for a while as I unpacked my belongings into the dorm room, and then I jetted over to the BCM that afternoon. They were having a celebration for the incoming freshman. It was a chance to meet other people and relieve the anxiety of moving to college.

The moment I walked into the building, Straight-Face was in his zone.

It was another religious crowd, and he was a pro at working these types of crowds.

He knew the lingo. He knew how to respond to things. He was on fire!

He had learned a lot since that first night of eating pizza with the youth group at fifteen. He had been to enough youth camps, worship services, and youth rallies to know how to fit right in with any Evangelical crowd. He was right at home.

Underneath that mask though, the real me was as intimidated as I have ever been. Since I had first arrived on the college campus, I had never been around so many cute guys at once. I was paying close attention to my eyes, making sure I didn't slip up and let them wander. But they were everywhere! On top of that, some of them were openly gay. Well, I assume they were. If they weren't open, they might as well have been. If they had their own Straight-Face masks, their masks were pretty defective because they weren't hiding it very well.

This was my first time being around openly gay people, much less ones who were my age and were smoking hot. It was really hard not to stare at them and adore them from afar, but I couldn't do that. Straight-Face wouldn't let me.

Do you really want to undo everything you've worked so hard for? What if someone sees you?

I knew he was right. I didn't want to undo everything. I mean, I really had worked hard. Too hard, actually.

After working so hard to try and make God love me, I had to protect that work. It became everything.

When people tried to undermine all of the work that I had put in to creating an alter ego, I would get defensive. I would hear about God's grace and how you can't buy God's love, but I didn't want to listen to them. I didn't even want to consider the possibility that they could be right, because that would mean all of my hard work (and wasted time) was for nothing.

Grace had become a four-letter word.

Besides, I had bigger fish to fry than to check out cute guys. Even if they did run around the frat houses with their shirts off. Those damn frat houses were worse than swimming pools, and I had to pass by them every day. Eventually, I found a new route to my dorm.

I made a few friends almost instantaneously at the BCM, and I was really enjoying my college experience. Even though I was intimidated, I had a deeper passion for fighting my homosexual urges, and I was preparing for the fight. The first weekend on campus had shown me how hard of a fight it was going to be, but I was determined. I decided I was either going to have to be all in, or not at all.

Monday came and I began my first classes. I tried to soak in all that was going on around me, but sometimes it was too much to take in. In the Student Union, every single club and organization were all lined up with their respective booths, each trying to get as many incoming freshman as they could.

Being a good, Evangelical boy, I made a bee-line to the College Republicans' booth. I didn't know much about politics, or even really care for that matter. But, when you are a budding Evangelical, there are three things you are supposed to love: Jesus, women, and Republicans. So, I made sure I was at least going to get two out of three.

Within a few short weeks, I had found myself as the president of the College Republicans, a freshman leader at the BCM, and coasting in my classes. Things were going smoother for Straight-Face than ever anticipated.

———————————

I settled into my classes, and made a stand in each one of them as "that conservative guy." I don't think they really enjoyed my presence a whole lot in a few of my classes, but I didn't care. I was "being a light for Jesus," and if they didn't like it, they could just suck it up. The older I got, the bolder I got. And the bolder I got, the more obnoxious I became.

Nonetheless, I was doing what I thought God wanted me to do.

So far, Straight-Face was running everything, and he didn't mind that at all. If he could have had total control, he would have taken it. He only had one obstacle that was holding him back: speech class.

I was in an Honors Speech Class, and I sat right beside a guy named Peej. On the first day of class, he sat down beside me and said hello with a smile. My stomach churned, but I came right back with a roaring greeting.

He looked Italian, had jet black hair, a nice smile, and was always laughing. He was a cute guy.

The first couple of class sessions, we made small talk. I had a crush on him, but Straight-Face would not let it be shown. But, wow, it was tough for me. Especially since every once in a while, under the table, his knee would touch mine. I didn't even know if he realized it or not, but it was driving me insane! Sometimes, I couldn't wait until the next class just to sit by him again.

The day it all changed, though, was when we were chatting in class before the professor showed up. He was talking to a girl friend of his that was sitting at the adjoining table. I wasn't really paying attention to their conversation until I overheard him talk about a date he had last weekend — with a guy.

As soon as he said it, my heart hit the seat that I was sitting in. My face went flush; my palms went sweaty.

Peej was an openly gay guy, and I had no idea. Here I was crushing on him as hard as I have ever crushed on anyone before, and he was gay, too. I gulped. Quickly, I regained my posture because I didn't want him, or anyone else, to see me like this. The entire class session, Straight-Face and I fought back and forth.

You know you can't sit here anymore, Straight-Face tried his hardest to convince me.

That's insane. I couldn't just move seats in the middle of the semester. That's weird.

If you keep sitting here, he retorted, *the temptation is going to be too much.*

I can hold my own. I've been doing great. No problems since I moved here.

Not yet, he said, *because you've been fleeing every chance you get. Remember: flee from sexual immorality! This is basic stuff!*

I reasoned that this would be illogical, and people would question my sudden change of seating. So, I continued sitting next to Peej. You can also rest assured that I never skipped that class.

About halfway into the semester, we were approaching midterms and were all chatting as class was ending.

"Hey, Peej, do you think you might want to try and get together and study for this thing? I have a feeling it's going to be tough," I said.

The words blurted out of my mouth before I, or Straight-Face, even realized it. I didn't even think about the words before I said them. It just kind of happened. Now, I was slightly embarrassed. I tried to take it back, but he replied too soon.

"Sure. I think that'd be great." He smiled back.

Woah? Really?

I knew this was going somewhere dangerous fast.

"Let me give you my number," he continued, "and you can hit me up sometime this week."

I put his number in my phone, and then gave him mine as well.

I was scared and excited at the same time. The real me was about to jump out of my skin with butterflies in my stomach, while Straight-Face was worried sick about where this was going to lead.

———————

I had had about enough of Straight-Face. Since I got to college, I had let him pretty much run everything. I had not allowed the real me any time to breathe. Since I was now in a dorm room with roommates, I had to keep the mask on at all times. The real me was beginning to burst at the seams, needing some time to myself. Luckily, though, I had been able to switch dorm rooms in the middle of the first semester, and that gave me a private room. After the class session where Peej gave me his number, I bolted back to my new dorm, bypassed my suitemates, and shut the door behind me.

I laid on my bed, and for the first time in months, I made Straight-Face shut up. I wouldn't let him get a word in. I just sat and thought about Peej. I thought about the possibilities of studying together — and more.

I don't know if I can put into words the feeling of a moment like that. It's the moment the first time a closeted person ever actually thinks about acting on their feelings. I think every person who has been closeted remembers his or her moment.

As I lay there, I pulled out my laptop and opened up Facebook. I typed in his name and found him almost instantly. I sent him a friend request and just scanned over his profile. I looked at his pictures and read his wall. I thought about how great it must be to be totally honest with the world about who you are. This guy held nothing back. His wall posts were about being gay, and his pictures did not hide this fact, either.

I remembered being a young teenager again, when I would sit and wish that I could live in a world where being gay was totally normal and accepted. I didn't think a world like that existed, or even ever really could exist. But the more I looked through Peej's life on social media, I began to realize that my dream was a reality for a lot of people. It made my head spin.

It was just a few minutes later that he accepted my friend request. The notification chiming through the computer speakers made my heart skip a beat. I looked at the chat menu, and he was online.

Should I send him a message? That would be okay, I think, *No harm in that.*

I was hesitant. He didn't know I was gay, and I didn't want to give him hints either, because I didn't want him talking about me to others. Especially if he somehow had friends who knew me, too. But, I also wanted to keep talking to him. I enjoyed talking to him. It was nice talking with someone my age who had the same feelings as I did, even if he didn't know I had those same feelings. I knew he did, and that was enough.

I finally decided I would say hi, but I would keep it casual.

I typed: "Hey bro!"

I sat.

I waited.

I was anxious.

In the old Facebook chat, you couldn't tell whether the other person was typing or not. You couldn't tell if they had even seen it or not. All you could do was wait.

What if he already saw it and ignored me? I bet he assumes I'm just a Christian jerk, and he probably doesn't want to talk to me.

But, finally, he replied: "Hey there :) What's up?"

I was as giddy as a junior high girl, and I didn't mind one bit. I wasn't going to let Straight-Face ruin this moment for me.

Me: "Nothing much at all. Just chilling in my dorm room. What about you?"

Peej: "Oh, that's cool. And nothing here either. Just got home."

I felt like an idiot. I didn't know what to say. I really wanted to just type, "I'm gay! Come. Here. Now." But I couldn't. Just talking to him was a big step for me. There was no way I could be honest about who I was yet.

Me: "So when do you want to try and get together and study?"

Peej: "I'm down for whenever. I'm pretty open."

What if he did suspect I was gay? I realized how easy he had given in to wanting to hang out with me, and he knew that I knew he was openly gay. So what if he wanted me as much as I was wanted him?

The thought really made the room spin. It also woke Straight-Face up from his forced slumber.

You're playing with fire here, he reminded me.

Nonetheless, I carried on the conversation with Peej while trying to ignore Straight-Face. I was amazed at how easy it was to ignore him if I really worked hard at it. I guess after years of hearing the same old lines, they begin to lose some effect.

Talking to him was quite nice, too. We talked about school, growing up in our respective towns, and what kind of movies we liked. I was actually talking to an openly gay guy that I knew in person, and it was flowing so naturally. More naturally than I had ever talked to a girl romantic interest, ever. I hadn't even noticed that not one, but several hours had passed.

Then, he started flirting a little bit.

Peej: "So, does a handsome guy like you not have a girlfriend?"

I had to pick my jaw up off of my computer keyboard. He just called me handsome.

What do I say to that?

Me: "Nah, not right now. I had one back in high school, but we broke up before I moved to college."

It was a bold-faced lie, but I figured it was a better option than telling him the truth.

Peej: "I understand."

Me: "What about you? Not dating anyone?"

Peej: "Nope. I'm a free man at the moment."

My curiosity was piqued. I saw my opportunity for questions, so I thought I would take it.

Me: "So, what do your parents think about you being gay?"

Peej: "They're pretty cool about it. My parents are laid back Catholics. They know it's not a choice, and so they just kind of roll with it."

Catholic, huh? This guys going to Hell for more than one reason.

Me: "Oh, that's cool. My brother is gay, too. My dad wasn't so cool about it."

Peej: "Yeah, that happens. It's unfortunate."

Silence.

Nobody knew what to say. I was getting more and more tempted to tell him about me.

I panicked.

When I panic, I resort to habit.

Habit was my mask, and Straight-Face was more than ready to step in, because he had already let this go on too long as it was.

Me: "You should come to the BCM worship service with me sometime."

What? Did I really just ask him to come to worship service?

I mean, I loved going to worship services. But why did I ask him? He was openly gay - and Catholic!

On the other hand, maybe I could get him to be an Evangelical Jesus follower, too.

Maybe we could be two, closeted gay Jesus-followers together? Maybe I could win real points with God if instead of living the gay lifestyle, I actually won more gays for God? It didn't work on my brother, but maybe it would work on him?

I really had no idea why I asked him that when I knew he would not be interested. I think it was part envy. Being a closeted, gay Evangelical for so long lead me to feel jealous of a lot of people.

I was jealous of successful, straight Evangelicals, because they seemed to have it all together, and they were everything I wanted to be. I envied their straightness.

But I was also jealous of openly gay people, too. I envied their lives. I envied the fact that they were living out who they truly were, and they seemed not to have all the pain that I did. I was pissed that God made it so hard to act on my feelings when it seemed so easy on them.

I began to bemoan the gay lifestyle, all the while secretly wishing I was living it. I applauded them in the back of my mind, while in my speech I detested the "abominable homosexuals." It's a very complicated place to be, to say the least.

This is why when given the opportunity, I invited gay people to church. I wanted to save their souls, but I also kind of hoped they would throw themselves on me. I hoped to find someone who was as serious about their faith in Christ as I was, but who also had the same sexual feelings I did.

That's probably why I invited Peej to worship. I wanted him to come and be around me, hoping that he would throw himself on me.

He respectfully declined my invitation, however.

I mean, I kind of expected it.

It also killed the conversation. I closed my computer and laid back down on my dorm room bed.

So, this gay actually thought I was cute. I knew I could probably at least kiss him, if I wanted to.

And that thought made my head very foggy.

Whenever I shut Straight-Face off for a while, he came back with a vengeance, and he was really good at a guilt trip.

You know you can't hang out with this guy! If you get in that moment, you're not going to be able to say no. And once you give in, you're done! There's no way God will use you for ministry if you do that! You're going to be headed straight to Hell. Everything you have worked for is going to go out the window.

I laid on my bed that night, rolling the conversation around in my head. Each time, Straight-Face came at me stronger.

Why are you doing this to yourself? God hates this. You're making God hate you!

As the guilt trip continued, I daydreamed again about a life where homosexuality wasn't wrong.

Why couldn't I live in a time where it's no big deal? Why couldn't God have just said this was okay? Why is it such a bad thing?

I thought about what that kind of life would be like, and I liked it a lot. It would be glorious.

The more I thought about it, the angrier I became.

Why shouldn't I have been angry? I had worked hard!

Really hard.

Really really hard.

God still had not taken it away from me, even though I had given him everything. All while growing up, I never partied, I never had sex. I never even used tobacco.

Nothing.

All for the sake of "being good for Jesus."

But where was God in all of this? Why had he not made me

straight yet?

Straight-Face felt like he must defend God.

You know that God loves you, right? He just wants what is best for you.

Straight-Face was programmed by the Evangelical church. Whenever doubts arose from the real me, he knew how to stop them dead in their tracks. But, this time, unlike before, I second guessed him.

Did God really love me like everyone said? I had done so much. Given so much. He didn't seem to be anywhere in the midst of this. I was starting to wonder if He even cared.

You know He does care about you.

How could I have known this?

Wait, maybe God doesn't care that I'm gay?

As soon as that thought entered my head, Straight-Face went nuts.

That's preposterous! You're being deceived by the Devil now, just like your brother! It's plain as day in Scripture, and God doesn't change. You know it's wrong to be gay, so you shut that up right now!

Well, if He cared so much about homosexuality, but hasn't fixed it for me by now, then apparently He doesn't care about me.

Okay, I can see I'm not getting anywhere on this. If you don't do it for God, at least do it for your parents. What would they think? Two sons who are gay? That would kill your dad. And what about everyone else? You've made so many great friends since you have moved to college, and they are all Baptist. Do you think they would hang out with someone who's gay?

I sighed because I knew he was right.

But what if they didn't have to know?

I pondered on that one for a minute, but of course Straight-Face had a response for that, too.

They will know. Your sins will always find you out. Numbers 32:23. They will find out, and you will be outcast. You will be done. Your life as you know it will be over. No hope for ministry. Ever.

And so, Straight-Face won again.

I finally resigned and went to sleep, letting Straight-Face have control again, for the sake of my soul and my sanity.

I never did hang out with Peej, either. Once Straight-Face won the argument that night, I just ignored him and acted like the conversation never happened. I figured that was for the best. But the temptation wasn't over just yet.

———————

A couple of weeks after that night, our speech class had to make an overnight trip to student congress at the state capitol. Two nights before we were set to leave, our professor gave us the room list. Of course, he paired me in a bed with Peej.

I was legitimately terrified.

If I shared a bed with Peej, the temptation would be too strong, and if I did anything, I knew Straight-Face was right — someone would find out.

I racked my brain. What was I going to do? I wanted to share a bed with him, but I knew I couldn't.

Flee from sexual immorality.

That was the verse Straight-Face kept bringing up. I knew I had to fight this. I had to flee from the situation altogether.

So, I called my dad on the phone. I explained to him that the teacher was trying to put me in the same room as a fag, and I didn't want to share a bed with him. He told me he would happily wire me the money to get my own hotel room on the trip.

I felt horrible, because I was sure that Peej knew I was avoiding sharing a bed with him because he was gay. I'm sure he thought I was scared that if I shared a bed with him, I'd get gay cooties, or that he would try to be all over me. In reality, I was scared of what I would do if we shared a bed. I felt bad, but I had to do what was the "Godly" thing to do, and as far as I was concerned, the Godly thing for me to do was to stay away from him.

Besides, I was heading to the capitol to fight for Creationism to be taught in public schools. I was president of the College Republicans, and I had to keep up appearances. Those appearances would be broken if the other people knew I was sharing a bed with a queer.

For some Evangelicals living in the conservative world, it is all about appearances. It's all about what things look like on the outside. You will do anything, and run over anyone, just to keep those masks on.

The Evangelicals have adopted a churchy phrase for not keeping up appearances: it's called "losing your witness." Your witness is what people see and think of you. It's others "seeing God in your life." If you do something less than Godly, and other people see it or know about it, then you have effectively "lost your witness." The thing is, if you lose your witness, you are then told you are no good to God's kingdom. If you lose your witness, you are told, people won't listen to you, and God can't use you to help them change their lives and walk away from sin.

I would do anything to protect my witness.

Chapter Seven

Buddha said, "To enjoy good health, to bring true happiness to one's family, to bring peace to all, one must first discipline and control one's own mind. If a man can control his mind he can find the way to Enlightenment, and all wisdom and virtue will naturally come to him." This sounds really nice and all, but by end of my first semester of college, I didn't have much control of my mind. As a matter of fact, I had pretty much lost control of myself to Straight-Face. While other people lose control of themselves to wild living during college, I had lost control of myself on the other end of the spectrum.

Straight-Face, who was just a puppet to my religion, made my decisions, controlled my speech, and guided my feet. He was taking over more and more. The only thing he hadn't had full control over was my thought life, even though he had tried. The real me was still hidden down inside.

Even though I quit talking to Peej because of Straight-Face, I couldn't shake the way I felt while I was talking to him. I enjoyed it. It reminded me of the times in high school when the mask would come off at night. But it was more real than that. I was actually connecting with another person.

Needless to say, it at least got my hormones going again. It had been a really long time since I had gone to the dark side of the Internet, but the temptation was too strong. I wanted to feel that again.

I closed my dorm room door, and turned on the computer. I knew exactly where to go to get what I wanted. I typed in the address and waited for the high-speed Internet to take me away.

However, only a minute or two into it, I was already bored. This just wasn't working any more. Since I talked to Peej, I knew that cheap sex was not what I was looking for - I wanted intimacy. I wanted to connect. I wanted someone to rip my mask off and remind me that I was real. So, I closed the computer and crawled back in to bed.

This caused my melancholy to come back, but even worse than in high school. I guess I had bottled the real me up so long that it finally just boiled over.

———————————

My cell phone vibrated on the desk beside my bed. The caller ID showed me that it was Mom, and I was tempted not to answer it because I wasn't ready to get out of bed yet. After a couple of more vibrations, I reached over and grabbed the phone.

"Hello?" I answered groggily.

"Hey, sweetie," she said. But, she was crying. Something was wrong. I rose up to the edge of the bed, not sure what to expect.

"What's wrong?" I fired back.

"Mrs. Lopez," she stopped to take a breathe in between sobs, "was hit by a train this morning."

My heart dropped. I didn't even know how to respond. I just sat there and let it sink in.

Mrs. Lopez was something of a heroine to me. She was my high school Spanish teacher who moved in to the house across the street while I was in junior high. She was a leftover hippie, who completely rejuvenated that old, condemned house into a sort of funhouse.

She boarded up the walls with recycled wood that she painted all different colors, built bookcases over the top of them, and filled the walls of her house to capacity with books. She took down all of her doors (including the bathroom door) and put beads in their place. She replaced white light bulbs with red and blue ones. She put a bathtub on her front porch, and built a fence all about her domain, with artwork and flowers hanging all over it. She put towels from all around the world on the ceiling of her house, and installed a stereo system you could hear for miles. Many days I would hear, quite plainly, Led Zeppelin or Pink Floyd resounding from her compound.

But as much as I enjoyed her eclectic house, that was not what drew me to her.

Mrs. Lopez had an infinite capacity to love people.

I would see it in her class while I was her student. She genuinely loved and cared for the kids in her class, no matter who they were, how smart they were, or where they came from. She wanted them to feel special; like they were the most special kid in the world.

Many days after school, I would go to her house and spend time with her.

I liked watching her. I admired her for the person that she was. I often debated telling her about my attraction to guys, but I never got the courage, because I was too busy denying it to myself. Instead, I played it out in my head often.

"Mrs. Lopez, can I tell you something?" I would say.

"Sure, hon, you can tell me anything." She would smile back. She always used to tell me this.

"I am gay." I would say, voice cracking, tears starting to well.

"Oh, honey, that's okay! There is nothing wrong with that."

"Really?" I would ask, looking up into her gleaming eyes.

"I love you just as much now, and maybe even more." She would say as she hugged me, "You know my love for you would never change, no matter what."

Then, I would hug her back, bawling my eyes out, because I would feel loved, assured, and secure.

But I never did tell her.

Maybe I didn't tell her because of the fear that possibly I was wrong, and I would rather hold on to the dream of who she was, instead of who she really was. I don't know. I did make up my mind, though, that if I ever did decide to tell someone, she was going to be the first. So, instead, I would just sit there with her. I asked questions. I read her philosophy books. I listened to her stories of traveling the world, meeting her lovers, and dropping acid. I listened to music with her and watched her close her eyes and soak in the words and the rhythm, allowing the music to take her back to a different time and place. I danced with her around the house. I cried with her when she was having a bad day, and I was there when she had her seizures. I watched the movies she gave me, I tasted the food she cooked, and I helped her with artwork.

I loved her.

This forty-something leftover hippie and I, a young closeted Baptist gay boy, were genuine friends.

I wanted to love like she loved. I wanted people to genuinely feel special when they were around me, too. But most of all, I really just wanted God to love me like she did.

I missed my chance, though. Mrs. Lopez was gone.

This gave my depression an excuse.

When you're stuck in the Evangelical world and closeted, you stay depressed a lot. But you can't tell anyone why you're depressed. So you look for reasons to give them. Well, I had my reason now. Not to say that I wasn't genuinely sad that Mrs. Lopez was gone. It's just now I had a reason that I could give everybody when they asked what was wrong.

Straight-Face tried to hide my feelings, but this time I wouldn't let him. This time, I told him to just shut up and let me feel for a little while. Surprisingly, he did.

The fact that I could get him to shut up like that sparked something in me.

Straight-Face didn't control me, even though I believed so heartedly that he did. I was letting him run my life simply because I was scared, but at the end of the day, it was just a mask.

Alter-egos are a powerful tool, but often, the two can start to merge. Unfortunately, the fake ego is the one that starts taking over more, because you get so used to playing a role. Eventually, a mask will make you believe that you can't live without it.

But in that moment, I was starting to realize that I gave Straight-Face too much control. I was losing myself inside this altar ego that was trying to please everyone else. I didn't have an identity. The only person others knew was Straight-Face. Nobody knew me. The real me didn't exist, except in my head, and I was more than tired of it. Here I was as an eighteen-year old, and had yet to have a true relationship with anyone, including family, because no one actually knew me.

I wanted to live in my own body, do my own things, say my own words. I didn't want to live Straight-Face's life anymore.

But what else could I do? I was stuck. I couldn't come out of the closet for numerous reasons.

For one, I believed homosexuality was wrong. Secondly, there's no way my dad could have handled having two gay sons. Finally, everyone around me would abandon me. Even though they didn't really know me, and I already felt alone, it was still all that I knew, and I didn't want what little inkling of relationships I had to go away.

So, I resorted to the Internet.

But not porn. Porn stopped working long ago. Porn was old news.

I had a webcam built into my computer, and it didn't take me long to find video chat rooms with guys my age, all of whom were gay.

I was hesitant at first, but then I started talking to them. Eventually, it was flowing as naturally as when I was talking to Peej.

I met guys from California, New York, England, Australia, and Canada. All over the world there were guys just like me, and I didn't have to wear my mask to talk to them. We really talked.

We talked about our hometowns, our families, our religions, and our hobbies. We talked about what we hoped to do with our lives, and if we were ever going to come out of the closet. We talked about who was cute and who was creepy. I was starting to connect with some of them in ways more true than I ever connected with people in real life, because they were connecting with me - not Straight-Face.

For a brief period, I was finally not suffocating behind that horrible, horrible mask.

For a brief period, I was breathing.

"What have I done? This is so wrong. I can't do this!" I muttered under my breath.

My innocent chat with a friend from just the next state over turned into something a little more than innocent - and Straight-Face was putting me on a guilt trip.

I had found such release in just chatting with these guys and being myself for a little while; why did I have to ruin it?

I knew I had opened up Pandora's Box. The feeling I got by talking with him was far more exhilarating than porn ever was. With porn, it was just me looking at someone else. But with this chat, it was someone's actually responding to me. It made me feel wanted, and gave me a hint of the intimacy that I had always craved.

I wanted more.

You can't do that again! If you keep doing that, God is going to get you!

I knew that, and I kept thinking about that. But as the next couple of days drug by, I began to not care.

I couldn't think of a reason to care, really.

I had given Him my entire adolescence, hoping that by the time I had reached adulthood, I would be straight. But nothing.

If anything, it had gotten worse.

What about all those verses where Jesus said that if you asked, it would be given? I had asked a million times, and I was still coming up empty-handed.

I stewed on this for a few days and became more frustrated every day.

Finally, I went back to talking to my friends online. It was the only place I found peace, and it was the only place on earth that I could put Straight-Face to sleep.

I had thought a lot about calling Peej. I had figured I had gone this far, maybe that would make me feel better, and I knew that Peej wouldn't tell anyone. Many times, I typed up the text, and deleted it before I sent it. I just couldn't take that chance, because I still knew ministry was my calling, and I really didn't want to hinder that.

At this point, I knew something had to give. The pain of losing Mrs. Lopez, the intense guilt of being gay, and the loneliness that college sometimes brings had all intensified, and I started diving into substances to try and numb the pain, or at least help me to escape reality for a little while. I tried tobacco, which helped with the stress of life, but not much else. Then, I had found a way to get alcohol. That seemed to help some, but eventually it wasn't enough. I remembered I had a Xanax prescription from when I was having anxiety attacks, so I started mixing that with the alcohol. Soon, this all spiraled into whatever I could get my hands on just to try and escape, even if for a few hours. My dorm room became my solace where I hid from the world.

In a matter of what seemed like days, I went from being the good Evangelical boy who never touched any of this stuff, to a reclusive user that barely left my dorm room.

I didn't know what else to do, though. Straight-Face had been in control for so long that I had forgotten how to live without him. Now that I had allowed myself to take him off for a while, I didn't know what to do. I just wanted to experience anything except life.

But the more I dove in, to both chatting with gay guys and substances, the more guilt ridden I became. It's true that I had been taking Straight-Face off when I was alone - which was often at this point, but that didn't mean that I didn't get to hear his numerous guilt trips about what I was doing with my life.

My moment of victorious breathing all at once turned into drowning.

———————————

Somehow, I still finished with good grades that first semester. I'm not sure how, because I barely went to class at the end. I packed my clothes and headed home for Christmas break. It was bittersweet. It was tough going back and seeing Monica's uninhabited hippie domain just across the road, but I was now around my parents, and so I needed Straight-Face to come back and run things, which gave me a little more stability. It put me back in the comfortable habit of hiding myself. I got through Christmas, and New Years was fast approaching.

I had picked up a job just to make some money during the break. One of the guys I worked with was a fraternity member at the same college I went to, and he had invited me to the New Year's party at his frat house. I wasn't really sure about it. I had never been to a "real" party in my life. When I was in high school, I went to a couple of bonfire, middle-of-the-field, low-key parties. But never had I been to a college frat party. That was a whole new world to me. But in my Xanax muddled reality, I really couldn't care less about much at that point. I really didn't want to go, but I felt like I needed something — anything — to snap me out of the depression.

On New Year's Eve, I loaded my car to head back to college. This particular frat was known for their wild parties of booze, pot, and loose women. I figured I was probably about to embark on all three. On the way though, I passed by my old church, and my old youth minister was out in the parking lot. He waved at me and motioned for me to come say hi.

I can't let him see me like this, I thought to myself.

But, he had already seen me, and I had already waved, so I couldn't just keep driving. I turned the car around and quickly scanned myself in the rear view mirror. My eyes looked old. Much older than eighteen. I don't know if it was a mixture of not sleeping or the Xanax, but they looked heavy. It was like the all-consuming guilt, sadness, and loneliness had taken up residence in the little pockets under my eyes, pulling them down into one droopy black hammock. I wiped my eyes and widened them, trying to pull myself together as I pulled into the parking lot beside him.

All right, Straight-Face, do your thing.

In an instant, the smile was painted onto my face.

But, I was a little out of practice, and Straight-Face was not putting 100 percent into his performance.

He could tell something was wrong, and before I knew it, we were in his office. I sat across from him, trying to hold it all together, but I just couldn't.

I found myself confessing to him how I had been living - minus the whole gay thing, mind you - and how I couldn't find an escape. It felt good to talk to someone, though, even if he was only getting part of the truth. I think my little rebellions had given me an excuse to just tell someone that something was wrong, and that I was hurting. Even if it was only for a brief moment, it was a moment of semi-authenticity, and was like finally coming up to breathe again since I started drowning.

Sitting in his office that night, I "rededicated my life to Christ." If you aren't familiar with Evangelicalism, there are a few different phrases you may not know. This is one of them. The term "saved" is more well known. To be "saved" describes the moment that you say a prayer for the forgiveness of your sins, and Jesus Christ's sacrifice on the cross saves your soul from Hell. In typical Evangelicalism, this is done simply by putting your faith in Christ and asking him to forgive you of your sins.

It's a single moment, marked with rejoicing and usually followed by a baptism.

However, unless you're a super saint, there are usually times when you will not always "live worthy of the life that you have received," and you "backslide." Backsliding is a term for falling back into the life of sin after you have been saved. Baptists believe that once you are saved, you are always saved. So, if you backslide, there is no sense in being saved again. So, they came up with another term of coming to Christ after you've already been saved. This is called "rededicating your life to Christ."

Most Evangelicals, especially if they grew up in the church, will do this probably a dozen times in their lives, if not more. As a youth, I probably did it at least three times a year, at just about every youth camp I went to. Now, as a college freshmen, I was rededicating my life to Christ once again.

I determined this time was the last time, though. I was tip-toeing around sin the entire semester, and it had left me with nothing but sadness and bitterness. It never crossed my mind that my depression was coming from repression, religious-filled guilt, or lack of love and intimacy in my life. Instead, I assumed all of my sadness was because my own sin was destroying my life, and facing my sin was the only way to fix that pain.

I was back in the Game.

I ended up spending that New Year's Eve with the youth group instead of going to the frat party, which was probably for the best. There is no telling where I would have gone with my life if I had not stopped and talked to my old youth minister.

After catching up on my sleep from New Year's, I went back to my bedroom at my parents' house. Everything over the past semester was playing through my head, and all of the stupid stuff I had done was haunting me. I know in the scope of most people's lives, my little rebellious stage was quite mild, but in my Evangelical mind, it was more than enough to send me straight to Hell and fill me with enough guilt for a lifetime.

Plus, I still had those damned homosexual attractions!

I had rededicated my life to Christ, but I was already doubting it. I was not doubting the existence of God, nor the divinity of Christ, nor any of the tenets of my Southern Baptist faith. Not in the least. I was doubting whether God actually wanted me or not, and this is one of the toughest things to doubt.

It's one thing to not believe in God; it's another to believe in God and believe that He doesn't love you or want you. That's a whole new level of despair, and it is a period that most gay Christians go through at one point.

I decided to put God to the test, and to give me a new foundation to build off of for the future. I was praying hard, weeping over my homosexual attractions. I asked God to give me some sense of His presence, or that He still wanted me. I had assumed He wouldn't want a gay guy.

I was on my knees down beside my bed, face down on the floor. My head was on the hard floor, so I just grabbed my Bible off of the desk, opened it, and laid my head upon the pages as a cushion. I just kept praying.

I asked God to show me something.

Anything, God. I promise I will give my life completely to You and to Your ministry, if You will simply just show me that You still want me. I know that I'm gay, but I haven't acted on that. I am trying really hard, too.

I'm sorry for how the last few months have been, but I'm ready to make a change. I'm ready to go in all the way with You, again. But, I need to know that You still want me. Do You still love me? Do I really belong to You?

I continued asking God for some way to know that He really did want me. I don't even know how long. I finally opened my eyes and rose up. My tear-filled eyes refocused, and I looked down at the Bible that I had randomly grabbed and opened up to lay my head on. My eyes focused and I saw this verse:

'I will give them a heart to know Me, for I am the LORD; and they will be My people, and I will be their God, for they will return to Me with their whole heart. (Jeremiah 24:7, NASB)

It sort of took me by surprise.

Now, I don't know if that was really God speaking to me or just a crazy coincidence. All I know is that in my mind, it was just the assurance that I needed. The prodigal son had returned. Straight-Face was coming back on for good, and my faith had been restored.

It was time to recharge and go to work for the kingdom of God.

Chapter Eight

I stared at the cork-board, taking in each notice and piece
of paper, one by one. The board was inside the Baptist Collegiate
Ministries, so everything on it was religiously based. It was a new
semester, and churches were posting job openings as they prepared for
the coming summer months.

I had already determined by the time I moved back into the
dorm for the second semester that I was going to begin approaching
ministry. I spent all of Christmas break getting my head back on
straight, getting away from any substances, getting to where I thought
God wanted me to be, and preparing for the rest of my life.

I did learn something from my first semester, though: I wasn't
changing. I had resolved that homosexual attractions are not something
that just "go away." I had spent the last decade trying to change those
feelings, but to no avail. Attractions are attractions, and you can't
change them any more than you can change your height.

I had made up my mind that I was going to give up the fight to try and change myself. I knew it wasn't going to happen, and the longer I tried, the more frustrated and bitter I would become toward God.

I did, however, decide that I was never going to live the lifestyle. I was adjusting to the idea of living a single life, for the good of my soul. If I did happen to find a woman someday that I could handle living with, then I would try and do the family thing. But, I wasn't going to actively look either. I was just going to focus on ministry with everything that I had.

One of the notices caught my attention. It was a Baptist-like, non-denominational church on the edge of town. It was a church of about two hundred people and about ten youth. They were looking for a college-aged, part-time youth minister.

I took down the number, breathed in a deep breath as I slipped on Straight-Face, and called the pastor. He asked me to come by that afternoon to talk to him.

It took only ten minutes to get there from my dorm. I pulled into the long driveway to a quaint little church set up off of the highway in front of a small patch of woods. It really was beautiful, especially the gardens and wooded area behind it. The pastor was about sixty years old and a jolly guy. We hit it off instantly as we talked about church, religion, and music. We both were musicians and that led us to talk about style of worship, which led to us talking about mission statements, which led to a host of other things.

After about an hour or so of talking, he smiled at me and said, "Well, I was going to interview more people, but I feel like you are the right guy for the job."

I didn't know what to say to that. It caught me off guard that he offered me the job just like that. I was expecting this to take weeks!

He stuck out his hand for a handshake, and I grasped his hand with a smile, affirming that I was accepting the job.

I was officially — finally! — in the ministry.

———————

I started at the church the following Sunday, and set right in doing ministry work. I was meeting the kids, learning the new people, and preparing for that summer's events. I really did have a blast doing what I was doing, and I felt pretty natural doing it. Straight-Face was having a heyday, and even more people were falling in love with him and his accomplishments.

I only had a small group of students, but they were a great group. We had a lot of fun times, and through that whole summer, I felt like we were really growing together.

However, my attractions still weren't going away. I knew that they wouldn't, but I couldn't forget them like I wanted so badly to do.

For so long, I had been focused on changing my attractions, and that's a lot different than trying to forget them.

When you're trying to change your orientation, it's okay to think about the fact that you have the attraction to the same sex. You have to monitor progress, and you actually stay more in tune with your attractions because you're focused on changing them.

When you're trying to forget your orientation, though, you don't want the attractions to even cross your mind. You don't want to focus on them anymore, and you want to ignore any reference to it. You want to erase all of it from your mind, and act like it's not even there.

But trying to forget your attractions is like trying to force yourself not to blink. It might work for a minute, but it doesn't work long. Attractions to other people are such a normal part of your life that it is impossible to forget about them without forgetting yourself.

That's where Straight-Face came back in to play.

I had tried to snuff him out just months before, but I needed him now more than ever. Before, I was fighting to keep my own identity while wearing the mask. Now, I was trying to lose myself within the mask, hoping that Straight-Face would eventually absorb all of me.

Unfortunately, no matter how much control I willingly gave to Straight-Face, the real me was still lingering inside of me, not letting the mask have it all. No matter how hard I fought it off, the attractions just weren't disappearing.

We went to youth camps that summer, we had weekend events, and plenty of time hanging out. We dove into Scripture together, and were building a good community amongst ourselves. We had grown from ten kids to about forty by Christmas, and things were going really well.

As I approached another New Year, I was quite pleased with where things had gone. Just this time last year, I was on the verge of insanity, trying to kill my sorrows with alcohol and Xanax, and feeling sorry for myself because I had same-sex attraction.

Now, I was in a conservative, Evangelical church, succeeding in ministry, and trying hard to forget my attractions.

In my estimation, I was winning the Game.

But, apparently not in everyone's.

I was in my dorm room watching television when my pastor called my cell phone.

"Hey, Brandon, I was wondering if you could meet me up at the church to talk?" he said, sounding like something was weighing heavily on his mind.

"Uh, sure. Give me about twenty minutes." I replied back, wondering what this was about.

I hung up the phone and threw my shoes on. My mind churned with possibilities.

Are they out of money and can't support me anymore? Did something happen to one of my students? Maybe it's not a bad thing? Maybe he just wants to talk about the future of the ministry? Or maybe he has ideas about something?

I traveled up to the church, where he was waiting for me. We sat down in his little den inside the church and went through typical formalities of asking each other how our days were going.

"So, what's up?" I asked, wanting to cut to the chase. I don't like letting my imagination ramble. I like knowing things as quickly as possible.

"Well," he started, "I don't want to offend you in any way. I want you to know that I love you and am here for you, and that no one knows about this conversation except for you and me."

Now my mind was really reeling, and I could feel my stomach turning over.

"Okay." I said, the word eeking slowly and unassuredly from my lips.

"Quite frankly, I feel like the Holy Spirit is telling me…" he paused and breathed heavily. The anticipation was killing me!

The last part of this sentence felt like it took about four years for him to spit it out. Finally he finished, "…that you are struggling with feelings of homosexuality."

It was official: my stomach did three back-flips, grabbed my liver to dance the Rumba, and decided to use my heart for a drum.

How did he know? I have spent this whole year not even thinking about my feelings? How could he possibly think that?

I was confused in more ways than one.

I could feel my face turning red. The way he said it was so blunt, and caught me so off-guard, that I just didn't know how to respond. I had practiced fifty other scenarios on the way to meet with him, but this wasn't even on the list. After what seemed like forever, Straight-Face started getting angry and defensive. He had worked so hard at hiding the real me, he was not about to go down without a fight.

I collected my thoughts, then mustered up everything within my power and came back with the most exquisite answer I could give: "What?"

"Well, I feel like I can sense that," he continued. "I don't know why. But I feel like that's what the Spirit is telling me."

"No, no!" scoffed Straight-Face, "I like women. Like, a lot." I may have overdone that statement, hands flying through the air with wild gesticulations, contorted eyebrows, and widened eyes.

Easy, Brandon. Don't overdo it. You'll give yourself away.

"Now, I didn't want to offend you. I just wanted you to know that if you are, you can be honest with me. I won't fire you or anything like that, and it can just be between us. I firmly believe homosexuality is a type of demonic possession, and that you can't help how you feel, and that if you are in fact dealing with this, then you and I can work together to heal you of it."

I just stared. I was afraid my silence was probably answer enough. So many things ran through my head in that moment.

Wow. Is he serious? Is this really happening? Should I just tell him? He sounds genuine. Maybe he really can heal me? But what if this is a trap? What if I tell him, and then he can't heal me? Then, I'm stuck and someone will know. He could blackball me from ever working in the ministry again! I just can't risk it. There is too much to lose. I just can't tell him.

"No...no," I finally concluded, "I promise I'm not gay. I don't know what gave you those vibes." I had settled by this point, but my face was still blushing, and I was sweating profusely.

"Nothing gave me the vibes," he reassured, "I just feel like that's what the Spirit has told me."

After telling him in twenty different variations that I did not have homosexual attractions, we closed the most awkward meeting of my life. We went about business as usual. But it didn't feel right after that.

I felt threatened. Vulnerable. Cut.

From that moment on, I felt like he knew, and so my whole insides were shaking every time I was around him. My year of trying to forget the feelings was nice, but it was definitely over. After the meeting, it was all I could think about. I churned in my mind over and over again how much I hated those damn attractions, and how - once again - they were messing up my life. The uneasiness was overwhelming, and I knew I had to get out of that place.

I was never angry at him, however. I believe he was as genuine as he could possibly be. He just wanted to help. But I wasn't in a stage of wanting help. I had passed that stage already. He could have offered that to me a few years before, and I would have taken it. But, I had already spent years trying to fix it, and it didn't work.

No, I didn't want help.

I wanted to hide.

———————————

After a few very awkward weeks, I was preparing a weekend event for my youth. I had wanted to do a treasure hunt during the weekend, and there was another minister in town who was known for making the best treasure hunts around. So, I found his number and called him up.

His name was Jeremy and he met me in town for lunch at a local Mexican restaurant. Over chips and salsa, we shot the breeze for a little while, and got to know one another. He was in his mid-thirties, and was a good-looking Italian guy. He was the college minister at one of the local churches, and I could tell upon meeting him that this guy was a leader. He was the type of guy who walked into a room, and everyone knew he meant business.

Jeremy spent the next couple of weeks helping me prepare for the event and even came out the weekend of the event to help me run the treasure hunt. We seemed to connect really well. During the treasure hunt, we sent all the kids out on their little adventure, and he and I had to stay behind at the church to wait on the kids to come back. This gave us about two hours to kill.

While we were chatting, he told me that at his church, there was a position opening up for youth minister intern. He said it was a much larger church of one thousand, with a youth group of about one hundred kids. He thought I would be a good fit, and asked he if I was interested.

"Heck yes!" I exclaimed, "I've been feeling for a little while now that my time here is done, and I was about to start looking for what was next."

Of course, I didn't tell him why I was feeling that way.

"That's great. I'll talk to the youth minister and see what we can do."

That next week, we met with the youth minister for lunch and talked. We chatted like old friends who had known each other for years, and Straight-Face was definitely giving his A-game.

By the end of the lunch, they had offered me the job. I accepted it instantly.

The next Sunday, after church, I told my pastor about the new job and he seemed a little heartbroken. I felt bad, but I knew I had to escape.

My fight or flight mode was turned all the way to flight. It was time to move on in life and try to escape my attractions once again.

Chapter Nine

I started at my new church on Mother's Day of 2008. I had never been in a church that size before, and it was all brand new to me. The sanctuary was huge. There were three wings to the building, and the youth took up the whole first four rows of the church.

I stood before the church as the pastor introduced me as the new intern who would be working with the youth group.

I looked out from the stage at the youth. Standing before this group of teenagers, I knew that they were wondering what kind of weirdo I was, or if I were going to laugh at their stupid jokes.

Right behind them, I could see the parent's eyes questioning me. I imagined they were wondering if they could trust me with their daughters, or if I was a safe enough driver for their sons to ride in my car, if I was actually going to teach their kids about Jesus and the value of saving sex for marriage, or if I was just going to make "yo momma" jokes with them, and throw water balloons in the church hallways.

Finally, I could feel the old ladies' eyes adoring me. Old ladies always had granddaughters lined up to marry Straight-Face.

Unfortunately for them, and fortunately for me, Straight-Face never did much marrying of granddaughters.

I got through the opening ceremonies, and luckily, since it was Mother's Day, the focus was more on the moms than on me. When you have a personality like mine, being in the closet can be a weird situation. I am an extreme extrovert, and I like being in front of others. Being on stage before hundreds of people does not faze me one bit.

But being in the closet, those moments were sort of ruined for me. I perceived – even though it was probably all in my head – that everyone out there knew. When I would preach, people would joke about how I moved around. I was like a Pentecostal preacher in that Baptist church, pacing back and forth on stage. I never used notes, so I didn't have to be behind a pulpit. As I talked I would sit on the altar, walk down the aisles, or prop up against the piano.

But I never stayed still. Not for long, anyways.

That's because I couldn't. I felt their eyes piercing my soul, and the anxiety was too much. I had to stay moving. I had to be on my toes, and I never, ever looked them in the eyes. Most of my preaching was done to the sound-board balcony that hung just above the congregation in the very back of the sanctuary.

I was perfectly fine with not being up front very long that first Sunday.

———————

I settled into the new ministry position quite easily. The youth minister, now my new boss, and I hit it off immediately. He was one of the funniest guys I had ever met, and we had a lot of fun together.

We would talk about camp while playing ping-pong and make stupid videos for the kids that we would show at the following Wednesday night youth worship service.

He was older than me, just passing forty, and he had a wife and two kids. I knew that there was a lot I could learn from him, and he quickly became a mentor figure for me. The thing that really stuck out to me about him was how authentic he was in everything he did. For the first time that I could ever remember, he was the same person around me that he was around the kids, and around the pastor. When I was over at his house with his family, he was the same person there as he was in front of a group of old ladies at church. He excelled at authenticity, and I realized how inspiring and alluring authenticity was. He was a guy who loved Jesus, but he didn't stop being human. He enjoyed life, and he made life more enjoyable just by being around him.

Needless to say, it was always a lot of fun working with him. On top of that, Straight-Face was back in his groove in youth ministry, and everything was going great.

My only problem was that I was once again craving that intimacy and the need to be real. Watching the youth minister thrive at authenticity — and being loved for it — created for a newfound hunger for reality that just wouldn't go away, no matter how hard I tried to repress it. I noticed that the longer I pushed away my feelings, the stronger they became. I started talking to guys online again. I kept it as innocent as I could, but it was so nice just talking to them. By this point, a few of them had become real friends, and we kept up with each other's lives.

Being yourself is the most powerful drug in the world. Just a small taste of it, and you're hooked.

It has the same problem as real drugs, though. Once I stopped being myself, and put the mask back on, I went through some serious withdrawals.

Even though I didn't want to go back to it and had worked so hard to keep Straight-Face on, once I had tasted it, it was too late. I had felt it run through my veins and I inhaled it all in. I had experienced the high of being myself, and I never wanted to come down.

The next morning, though, was worse than any hangover I've ever had. Straight-Face came screaming back at me, harder than before.

Are you kidding me? What are you getting yourself into? You know this is wrong. You are playing with hellfire, kid. You're an abomination. You really want to act like one of those faggots? Do you really want to live like that? With everyone hating you?

I would sit back and let Straight-Face give me his verbal beat down. I knew I deserved it. I knew this was part of it. I had screwed up. I had let my sinful passions take over, and now I had to pay the consequences.

The guilt was always so heavy.

I truly wanted to please God. I really wanted to do what I thought God would want me to do. That is mostly the reason why I hid in my closet, and made my home there. I only wanted to make God happy.

The only thing I had ever heard in my whole life was that being gay was an abomination, and I could not make God happy and live the gay lifestyle. I had settled in to the fact that my life was to be spent alone. It wasn't the best case scenario for me, but I assumed it would be better to live alone and get to heaven than to live for myself and go to Hell. It was just that simple. I would sacrifice my life in the here and now, and await the rewards when I got to Heaven. Songs like "In the Sweet By and By" became my anthem to life.

But, some of these guys I was talking to online didn't think that way. I talked to people who had a completely different theology, and it piqued my interest.

For the first time in my life, I began to second guess some things. I had the thoughts before, especially when my brother came out, but I always pushed them away. Now, though, I was forming some real friendships with people who thought the same way as my brother, and I wasn't sure what was true anymore. I wondered if I was wrong, if what I had been taught wasn't true and that God really had made me this way.

What if I was missing out on the life God had for me by living in the closet?

Questions like these began to haunt me. What if all of my sacrifice had been for nothing? What if it was not at all what God wanted for me?

Not too long before, I would have gotten defensive at that thought, because I wanted to protect all of my work. But I couldn't escape those thoughts, so I finally embraced them and truly began to ask myself — and ask God — those questions.

Straight-Face would always try to shut those thoughts up, and sometimes he would win. But they always came back, and were coming back more frequently.

———

My life had become a cycle by this point. I would wake up in the morning, pray diligently for God's forgiveness for being gay and talking to other gay people about it online, go to school and work, study Scripture, help the youth minister with whatever he needed, spend the afternoon hanging out with my church friends and students, go home, get online, talk to my gay friends, then go to sleep.

Wash. Rinse. Repeat.

It was my routine.

My nighttime talks had become my sanctuary. It was a time when I could take the mask off and be myself. My nights became a time where I wasn't who other people wanted me to be.

It was the place I fed the hunger to be myself.

The real me scared me, though. Reality, in general, scared me. What scared me was how much I loved being me because I wasn't supposed to love being me. I was supposed to hate who I was because I was an abomination to God when I was really myself.

But, I just couldn't stop. I had become an authenticity junkie.

Nevertheless, I would have moments where the guilt was too much for talking to these other gay guys, and I would stop. Sometimes for days. Sometimes for months. But I always went back, because when I stopped, the hunger for being real was too much.

Music had become a huge part of my life, as well. I mean, it had always been important to me. I took piano lessons when I was around ten, and I picked up guitar at thirteen because of my Bob Dylan obsession. Throughout my teenage and college years, I picked up other instruments and learned them: bass, drums, dulcimer, harmonica, and whatever else I could afford to get my hands on.

But now, writing the songs, more than playing the music, was becoming more important. I was able to put into music all of the thoughts and feelings I couldn't really portray any other way. Especially when it came to guilt.

I wrote some really, really dark stuff during this time. Mostly, they were prayers to God. Sometimes, they were songs expressing anger toward God. Other times, they were prayers of earnest repentance and begging forgiveness. They were very personal, and most of these songs, no one has – or ever will – hear. They were between God and me.

Because of my newfound love of songwriting, I fell in love with a Christian musician named Rich Mullins. Rich quickly became my hero of the faith. He was so blatantly honest with his music and wrote powerful songs of worship about authenticity, the nature of God, and God's love.

Most of the time, I didn't believe what Rich was saying, but I really wanted to. So, I kept listening.

He had already passed away by the time I started listening to him, but it became a daily thing for me to listen to him, absorb his words, and try to figure him out. I began reading about his life, and he became even more of a hero of mine.

Rich Mullins was not your "average Christian." Here was a man who was making loads of money through his music; but yet, he lived, in his own words, like a ragamuffin. He only took as much as he needed to live (which wasn't a lot) and gave the rest away to charity. He could have been living in a huge house anywhere he wanted to, yet he was living in a trailer on an Indian Reservation in New Mexico, where he often walked around barefoot, playing games with the children on the reservation.

The more I dug in, the more Rich intrigued me. He loved his tobacco. He didn't mind dropping a cuss word. He even enjoyed a drink or two. But he loved God. That part was unwavering. He understood the gospel in a way I never thought possible, and it intrigued me so much that I had to learn more. There was something raw about Rich that drew me into asking more questions. The life of Rich Mullins pointed me to the gospel in a fresh, new way.

I learned, through studying his life, that one of his personal heroes was Brennan Manning, a Christian author. He was such a fan of Manning, that Rich was actually photographed on the cover of Manning's most popular book, The Ragamuffin Gospel, which is also where Rich got the name for his band — The Ragamuffin Band. Therefore, as soon as I learned this, I had to read this book. I thought that maybe it could give me some insight into this gospel that Rich seemed to have that I didn't. At the least, maybe it could help me to dive deeper into the faith. At the most, maybe it could actually help me with my lifelong struggle of homosexuality.

I jetted off to the nearest bookstore and bought a copy.

That night, I dove in and devoured everything that was being thrown at me. Soaking in Manning's words was refreshing and comforting. Everything Manning was telling me was in complete opposition to everything I had been taught about who God is. At first, it seemed more like a fairy tale or wishful thinking. But the more I read, the more it began to make sense.

Manning was proposing a God who loved me, which is the one thing I had always hoped for and tried my best to make happen.

The kicker was that Manning was saying I couldn't work to make God love me.

His entire version of God was completely different from mine.

His was a God who was passionately, deeply, and thoroughly in love with His creation - of which I was one. This was a God who willingly gave of Himself for my own soul, and stepped off of His throne to become one of us, just for the sake of leading me to true, real life.

This was a God who wasn't angry with me.

He wasn't mad at me.

He was pleased with me.

He loved me just as I am.

I soared through the book and took a step back as I finished it.

It rattled my brain. I wanted so badly to believe it. I wanted to know this God. I wanted it to be true!

But I just couldn't.

I had been taught for so long about a totally different God; a God who (kind of) loved me, as long as I was doing what He wanted me to do. The God I knew loved who I was supposed to be, but hated who I was, and unless I could become who I was supposed to be, then I was doomed for an eternity of punishment.

The new perspective of God was like tasting fruit after only ever eating vegetables. It was sweet and refreshing, and it made me wishful that this concept of God could be true.

I just wasn't convinced. Not yet, anyways.

Manning introduced this God, but didn't really give me much theological backing to support it. He simply left me craving for this loving God to be real.

Nonetheless, it led me to ask more questions.

———————

I now realized why many Evangelicals did not like to ask too many questions; once you start, it is hard to stop. When you find the answer to one question, it just leads to another question. I was quickly spiraling into this, and I had no idea what was going on.

I talked to my boss, the youth minister, about Rich Mullins and Brennan Manning, and what I had been reading, and he told me I should listen to a guy named Steve Brown. Steve had a radio show that aired every week, and he also had written a number of books about this very topic. Once again, I set out to the bookstore, picked up a copy of "Scandalous Freedom" by Steve Brown, and began reading it.

I couldn't believe it. I couldn't believe that I was actually believing what I was reading.

Steve was proposing the same God that Manning had written about, but Steve was giving me much more Scripture and theology to back it up. On top of that, Steve took it a step further: he was telling me that not only did God love me for who I was, but that God even liked me.

That was the boldest statement I had ever heard, and it took me a while to wrap my head around it.

I understood God's loving us. I mean, He made us. Even though I didn't believe it a lot of times, I at least understood the theology of a God who loved His creation.

But for God to like me? That seemed to take things too far, into a far too dangerous place. It seemed sacrilegious, even.

Steve talked about Christ and what Christ accomplished in His birth, death, and resurrection. He talked about how in Christ, we are completely, utterly, and totally free.

This concept of freedom captured my mind. I had experienced small doses of freedom before: freedom from Straight-Face, freedom from judgment, and freedom from self-hate. Even if I only experienced it in brief moments, I had at least experienced it.

I wanted to know more about what Steve was saying.

That whole summer, I dove in headlong to understanding this new God who I had learned about. Steve Brown had a series of podcasts based on the book in which he talked more in depth about what he was saying. I spent every afternoon going for walks and listening to Steve's podcasts.

I was learning, through Steve and others, that I needn't fear God, because it is not fear that God wanted from me - it was simply a relationship. Steve was telling me that I could go to God just as I was, which was such a bold thought that I once thought it unimaginable.

Usually, when I prayed to God, it was Straight-Face talking. The only time I would bring up being gay was when I prayed that God would forgive me for my attractions. That was it. But now, Steve and Brennan were telling me that I didn't need to wear the mask to talk to God. God wanted to talk to me.

It took a while, but eventually what Steve was saying was starting to sink in, and I felt the gospel move in me in ways I never thought imaginable. Scripture opened up for me. The book of Romans, the Letters from John, and especially Galatians, all seemed to carry a completely different weight than they did before. Words like grace, mercy, joy, peace, and love, all started making more sense.

I was in love with grace, and God was in love with me.

The clouds were whiter. The trees were greener. Life, in general, had gotten more beautiful than I thought was possible. By the end of that summer, I was a new man.

I was a new man in the sense that I had a real sense of joy about me, and it wasn't just Straight-Face that was smiling – the real me was smiling, too.

I was digging more and more into Scripture, because I was seeing things I had never seen before. As fall approached, I was reading more about Christian history and how the Bible was formed. I took an independent study with one of my philosophy professors about early church history. I began to read about how they canonized Scripture, about the lives of the early church fathers, and the early Creeds. My faith was growing deeper, and I could feel God tugging at my heart, pulling me deeper and deeper into grace and love. It was heavenly. Literally.

Not everything was happy and cheery, however. The youth minister and the pastor were not seeing eye-to-eye on a lot of things. Well, not on anything, really. It was making the work environment a pretty brutal place to be. I felt bad for the youth minister. He had become a friend and a mentor to me. He was like an older brother. I hated to see what he was going through, but I felt powerless to help.

By the time another New Year was upon us, he told me he was planning on leaving. I was devastated, but I saw it coming, too. I knew that things were changing, and that I had better be prepared for the ride.

Chapter Ten

If there is one thing that happens when you begin to understand grace and love for the first time, it is that it will make you fall in love with mission. For me, it was specifically homeless missions.

I don't know why I fell in love with homeless missions. I think part of it was because Rich Mullins talked a lot about the poor and serving Christ by serving them. Other parts of me think that it's because inside, I felt homeless. I felt like I was alone because of my attractions, and I felt almost hopeless in the fact that there was no escaping. I didn't really feel at home anywhere. Another part of me was just convinced that God had given me a heart for it, just because God wanted to do so.

Either way, I wanted to do homeless mission work. The problem was that there wasn't really any place to do that in the small city I was in. I did some digging, got the permission from my pastor, and I planned a mission trip to Dallas, Texas, for some of our college-aged guys and myself.

Straight-Face was still in charge of my life at this point. I was doing a lot better at squelching my attractions and keeping myself hidden. I was still on the grace high at that point and put all of my focus into learning as much about this newfound theology as I could. I still had nights where I had intense yearnings for intimacy, but I chalked those up to needing to purge my soul. I gritted me teeth through the loneliness of those nights and pushed through to the next day.

Right after the start of my senior year of college, eleven other guys and I loaded into our church van and headed to Dallas.

It truly was a life-changing trip, for more than one reason.

I had never been exposed much to the life of the homeless until that trip. But, I sensed that it was where I was supposed to be at that moment. The twelve of us went right to work and worked for a whole week. We worked at shelters, clothes closets, and food pantries. We gave out meals and stood with people who had no place to go in this world.

The greatest part about the trip, though, was the friendships I built while there. When you go and serve with other people, you can't help but bond with them. Personally, I think this is what God had in mind for the church, and this is why the early church was such a tight community.

When you serve alongside another person, the Spirit bonds you together in a very unique way.

We stayed up for hours at night, talking about the gospel and about our faith. All of us were discovering the gospel in a new way, and I was sharing with them the amazing things that I had been learning over the past summer. They seemed to be intrigued with this as much as I was. I was learning that I wasn't the only Evangelical looking for something deeper than what we had always been taught.

We had been there a week at this point, and were about to load up the van to take the long trip back home. I groggily woke up and checked my phone which was plugged up across the room. I saw about ten text messages on my phone, all from people at the church.

"He resigned this morning!" each one of them resounded. I stopped for a second and let that sink in. My mentor and my boss — my friend — was leaving. I knew it was coming because of the ongoing struggle between the pastor and him, but it still was disheartening.

I told the group of guys what was going on, and they all were as saddened as I was. It made for a long trip back home.

Once we got back home, I started talking to the church leadership. The youth minister had recommended that I take the job, and the church seemed to be on board with that idea. They were going to start me as an interim and let it grow from there.

But I was having some serious doubts.

In a sense, it was everything I wanted. I wanted to be a minister in a vibrant church where I could do ministry work and help lead students to Christ. I wanted to share everything I had been learning. I wanted them to know this God of grace because I knew many of them were taught the same things that I was taught growing up.

However, I wasn't sure I could handle the pressure.

Even though I was truly in love with Christ and the message of the gospel, there was still that whole "being gay" thing. As much as I wanted it to go away, it still hadn't. I tried to control it, but it was still there.

The older I got, the less I trusted myself.

I was scared I was eventually going to be outed, somehow or someway. The way my last pastor sensed that I was gay kept me on edge, and I always felt I was on the brink of being found out. I was scared I would slip up some day, and that it would get out, which would leave those kids feeling crushed, confused, and — God forbid — they lose their faith. That scared the hell out of me.

I did a lot of praying on it, and thought hard about whether I wanted to take this job or not.

Finally, after a few days of despairing over the decision, I met with Jeremy. He, too, knew about the conflicts between the youth minister and the pastor, and I knew I could talk to him about my own decision.

"So, what do you think?" he asked, as he sat across the table from me at a local coffeehouse.

"Well, I'm not sure. I mean, being in the ministry is the only thing I have ever wanted. I already know the students here, and we get along great. I guess I'm just scared at failing, somehow."

I couldn't tell him why or how I was scared of failing, but I could leave it vague enough to get a response from him.

"How would you fail?" he asked.

That is not the question I wanted him to ask.

"I don't know," I lied, "I'm just scared of not being good at it. What if I do it wrong, or teach them wrong, or something like that?"

"Brandon, we all have those fears. That's part of the job. You need to remember that you aren't going to be perfect. You're simply stepping with faith into a calling. Really, that's all you can do. God doesn't use perfect people for a reason. He uses people with flaws, and he uses people that don't know what in the hell they're doing. That's just how he works."

I knew he was right. I had read enough of Scripture to know that all of the saints of the past were pretty screwed up. This gave me hope. Maybe this is exactly what I was supposed to do.

After I left the meeting with Jeremy, I kept turning his words over in my head. I decided to put faith in the fact that God was going to do with me what he wanted to do with me, and I just had to step out and pray that I didn't screw it up.

In the words of singer Roger Waters, "What God wants, God gets. God help us all!"

I mean, I had no plans of coming out. I didn't even have plans to act on my attractions in anyway at all for that matter. So, why should I let that hold me back? I remembered Paul's words about having a "thorn in the flesh" (2 Cor. 12:7), and I figured this was just another part of following God. In the same way that Paul had to repress whatever his thorn was in order to do ministry, I needed to do the same.

Plus, I had always felt called to ministry. I felt God was leading me to share what I had learned about the Gospel, and this was my chance to do it.

I decided to take the job.

I was a full-time minister in the Southern Baptist church.

The thing about being a minister in the Evangelical church, or any church, I presume, is that you are expected to have all the answers. The problem is, you don't.

In fact, as a minister, you probably have more questions than the people in your ministry. If there is one thing I have learned from studying Scripture, it is that the more you study Scripture, the more you realize that you don't know anything.

But, since I was expected to have the answers, I acted like it.

Another thing about being a minister in the Evangelical church, especially the Evangelical church, is that you are expected to be near perfect. The problem is, you aren't.

In fact, as a minister, you most likely have a bigger propensity for sin than some of the people in your ministry, which is a well-kept secret. As the minister, you're expected to be perfect, so in the areas that you aren't perfect, you learn how to hide it. Once you get good at hiding it, the temptation to fall into sin grows even more, because you know you can hide it.

Some ministers don't have to start wearing their own masks until they become ministers, but I had lived my life with Straight-Face, so I was used to it. I knew I had to up my game, however. I had to be who they wanted me to be. Not only for the sake of the ministry, but because this was now my livelihood. If my mask came off, it wouldn't just be about my pride anymore – now I would be without a job. On top of that, whenever you are engulfed in full-time ministry, about 99 percent of your friends are going to come from within the church. That ups the ante even more. If Straight-Face were to come off, not only would I be full of shame, and not only would I be without a job, but I would proba- bly be scorned by all of the people whom I called "friend."

That was not helping my anxiety and paranoia at all.

But, I knew the risks when I took over the ministry.

I was prepared to storm the gates of Hell with the message of grace for my students.

My theology had grown so much over the past year, and I was eager to share what I had learned. I had learned that following Christ was about our love for God and for other people. I had learned that it was better to give than to receive. I had learned that grace was better than unforgiveness, love was better than hate, and that community was something we all craved, and something God wanted for us, as well.

As I formulated the pattern for the youth ministry, I revolved it around four main points. Everything we did had a reference to one of these points. The points were a summation of all I had been learning about grace and the Gospel.

Number 1: Through Christ, We Have Freedom.

This was essential. This was step one, and a person had to get this to fully understand the Gospel and to go deeper into the faith. Christ had come to set us free (Gal. 5:1). This freedom literally means that – freedom. As Steve Brown put it:

"You are really and truly and completely free. There is no kicker. There is no if, and, or but. You are free. You can do it right or wrong. You can obey or disobey. You can run from Christ or run to Christ. You can choose to become a faithful Christian or an unfaithful Christian. You can cry, cuss, and spit, or laugh, sing, and dance. You can read a novel or the Bible. You can watch television or pray. You're free...really free." (*A Scandalous Freedom*)

I understood my freedom when I began to understand just how much God cares for me and loves me, and that I was considered his beloved and adored child. When I realized that this love couldn't be taken away from me (Rom. 8:37-39), it caused me to fall even more deeply in love with God. I began to realize that this freedom meant that I could be totally real with God, because he is going to love me, no matter what — no matter what others thought about me, or even what I thought about myself. As Brennan Manning says in *The Wisdom of Tenderness*, "Real freedom is freedom from the opinions of others. Above all, freedom from your opinions about yourself. "

Christ set us free from the law, from religion, and from everything that could possibly hinder us from coming to God and letting Him love us.

It is freedom in the truest meaning of the word.

Complete and total refreshing freedom.

Number 2: The Freedom in Christ Leads to Authenticity.

Authenticity means being completely genuine and real. You have to learn your freedom in Christ before you can be authentic, however. But, because of the newfound freedom that we receive by Christ Jesus, we are able to be totally real with God.

We don't have to hide from Him anymore, because He is not out to get us. God loves you just as you are, and meets you where you are. He calls you his beloved son or daughter, and wants you to be as real with Him as you can be.

In fact, being with God and understanding the immense freedom we have received in Christ, he calls the real us out from behind our masks. We are drawn to being totally real with him. All other labels don't seem to matter anymore. All that matters is that we are God's children. To quote Manning again, "Define yourself radically as one beloved by God. This is the true self. Every other identity is illusion."

An amazing thing happens, though, when you begin to be totally authentic with God: you begin to crave authenticity with other people as well. It sort of boils over.

And why shouldn't it?

If you don't have to hide anything from the Creator of the universe, then why should you hide it from others? If you are able to be yourself with God, why not be yourself with your friends? And once you are authentic, you want to be authentic in every other area in your life. It all starts with opening up to God and letting Him reveal to you that He loves the real you, which He will do if you allow Him to. Once that happens, you want to know if this is true for other people as well.

Once you begin to be authentic with other people, and experience the love that comes from that. Your courage begins to build, and you want to be authentic with almost everyone. It's an amazing feeling, unlike anything else.

Being authentic is the natural outpouring of being free.

Number 3: Authenticity Leads to Transparency.

Once you become truly authentic, both with God and with other people, transparency naturally follows.

Some think that transparency and authenticity are the same thing, but they aren't. There is a key difference. Authenticity is being real with other people. It is a one-way action. Transparency, however, is a two-way street.

Transparency happens when you are authentic with people long enough that they begin to really understand you and know how you "tick." Once you've been authentic with people long enough, they are able to read you. It also works visa-versa. The reality is that once you're authentic with people, they begin to be authentic with you.

You both learn each other.

You understand each other.

You hear each other's stories.

You grow together.

You get inside each other's heads.

This is transparency.

And transparency is important.

Ultimately, transparency leads to true community.

Number 4: Transparency Leads to True Community.

I would dare say community is one of the main things God wants for us in this life. I think community is wrapped up within the wide-scope of what salvation is. Much of the New Testament is about community, whether that be the importance of it, how to live in it, or how not to live in it. Many writers of Scripture have something to say about community. From the writer of Hebrews compelling his readers to not giving up gathering together (Heb. 10:24-25), to Solomon gently reminding us that many people working together is better than one person working alone (Ecc. 4:9-12), Scripture is teemed with authors helping us see the importance of community.

The kingdom of God revolves around community. Living in the kingdom is stepping into the community of other believers, but it is not just about being one of them. Community is much deeper than that, and it doesn't come until transparency does.

With transparency, you learn the other person. With learning other people, you can understand when they are truly hurting or when they are truly happy. You can read when they are just blowing smoke or when they are telling the truth.

However, community takes that one step further. Whenever you sense another hurting, you lend a hand to help them. Whenever you sense another rejoicing, you rejoice with them. Community is taking what you learn via transparency, and applying it. You take what you learn, and you put action to it.

When someone you are transparent with needs a hug, you hug them. When they need a dollar, you give it to them. When they are so happy that they are brimming with excitement, you high five them.

When they are crying, you hold them. That's just how it works.
I think this fills God with joy when we do this.

We are commissioned to go out and be the hands and feet of
Christ. This is how that command is accomplished.

Whenever you hug another, you are being the arms of Christ.

Or if you give someone food, you are being the hands of Christ.

Maybe they have screwed up and they need to know they're
forgiven, so you speak forgiveness into their life. When you do that, you
are being the mouthpiece of Christ.

Christ is able to continue his ministry through the community
we build with one another. It is the ultimate plan of the Church, whether the Church of today realizes this or not. God works through the
community of believers, by the believers working together to be a part
of the ministry of reconciliation (2 Cor. 5:18).

———————————

I modeled everything in my new ministry around these four
principles. From the Wednesday night sermons, to the camps, to small
group meetings, I was focusing on one of these areas. This is what I
planned on teaching the students for however long I was going to be
here.

Even though I wasn't living out this spirit of authenticity that
I was so vehemently teaching, I believed that it was important that the
message got into the students. They needed to know, and I made it my
mission to make sure that they did.

Chapter Eleven

If there is one thing youth ministry taught me, it's that teenagers respond to grace.

I had always been taught a hellfire-and-brimstone Gospel while growing up, even into my college years. Honestly, a lot of teenagers do respond to that — in the moment. It leads to mass altar calls, with students crying their eyes out, weeping for God to save them from judgement.

However, it just doesn't stick for most of them. Statistics have shown us for the last decade, when students hit the age of eighteen, a majority of them leave the church — some of them for good.

But grace. Well, grace is a different story.

Grace excites teenagers, instead of filling them with fear. Hellfire and brimstone saps their energy from them; grace gives them joy.

The gospel of judgement makes kids scared to go to God; the gospel of grace leads them to their heavenly Father, their Abba. I have learned, though, that this doesn't apply only to teenagers. This applies to all people. It just took a while for me to figure it out.

The fact of the matter is that condemnation leads to death; grace leads to life.

Even though it doesn't lead to masses coming down to the altar, making big decisions for their lives only to give up on those decisions weeks later, it does lead people to make transformations in the way they live their lives, and it sticks with them for the long haul.

Judgment and condemnation are things that they see everyday in the world, while grace and love are quite rare. Grace and love intrigues people and draws them. The true gospel of Jesus Christ is so counter-cultural to most of us, that when we do go in, we have to go all in.

I was watching this happen everyday as I began to preach grace to these teenagers.

I took them back to Dallas, where I had gone the year before. This was the first trip we took as a youth group, and I could see their eyes opening in new ways while we were there.

I was trying to teach them the beautiful things that I had learned, and it was starting to stick with a lot of them.

But, I must say, I wasn't teaching them everything I was learning.

I had begun to dig deeper into some of the more liberal writers that I was always told to stay away from, simply because they were dangerous. As I read them, though, I was beginning to believe they weren't dangerous to me or to my faith; they were dangerous to the agenda of the people who told me to stay away from them.

I learned that if leaders are scared of their followers reading something else, it means they are insecure in their own message. If little things like facts and opinions can completely undo everything they have founded their faith upon, then you might want to be wary of that foundation yourself.

Evangelicalism, in general, seems to be afraid of doubt. Doubt disrupts everything it is working towards. Most of Evangelicalism is about certainty. It is about knowing that you know that you know that you are saved by the sacrifice of Christ and if you don't know that you know that you know that you are saved by the sacrifice of Christ, then you are in danger of spending all of eternity burning in a pit of everlasting fire. This is a real statement that I have heard many, many times, and have even said a few times myself.

Through reading progressive Christian writers like Brian McLaren and Rob Bell, I began to realize that doubt was not such a bad thing.

But this started getting Straight-Face all worked up. He began firing back about all the verses that talked about having faith, and if you waver in your faith, then you're in trouble. So, that sent me on a loop of trying to figure out who to believe.

My best friend, Kirstyn, gave me some profound words one day while I was trying to piece all of this together.

I told her about all I had been reading and what it was doing to my faith. She glanced across the dinner table and said, "The opposite of faith is not doubt. The opposite of faith is certainty."

I didn't even have to think about it. I knew she was right. Faith means that you are hoping for something, without knowing if it really is going to happen or not. That's the very definition of it. If you are certain about something, there is no room for faith. I lay my faith in the hope that love will win in the end, and that Jesus will be victorious. But, there is no way for me to be certain about this. Doubt is just a natural part of faith. At the end of the day, you just have to pray, "Lord, I believe. Help my unbelief."

I continued digging into these writers who I had always been warned against reading, and the part that surprised me – and sort of

117

angered me – was that they were making sense, more sense than the things I had always been taught. The things I was reading were lining up more with what Jesus taught than anything I had previously heard or read before.

There was no way I could share this with my students, though, as I would have been questioned by my pastor about what I had been reading. Luckily, I did have a group of friends who were my age, and we were reading this stuff together.

There were eight of us in all. One of them was my roommate, and one of them was my best friend, Kirstyn. The rest were in the college ministry at the church or had gone to college with me. We were all raised in the Evangelical church, and after some talking, we all realized we were asking the same questions. A lot of these people were some of the same who went to Dallas with me. We began meeting, semi-secretly, once a week, and discussing these topics, going back to Scripture, and praying together.

In a short amount of time, we had begun forming a community unlike any we had ever been a part of before. In fact, we called our little group *Kehila*, which is the Hebrew word for "community."

The more we met, the confusion I was feeling grew stronger. One side of me really wanted what I was reading to be true. It just made more sense than all of the things I had been taught my whole life. The way God was, the way we were to interact with him, and the role of Scripture, all of these things were reexamined and put into this new light in such a way that made all of theology just meld together almost seamlessly. Even though it left room for a lot of mystery, it still made sense.

I'm not going to lie and say all of me wanted it to be true, though, because it was very uncomfortable. I knew that if I ever took that step into fully believing it and applying what I was learning, then my life was going to turn completely upside down. I knew that it was risky and would eventually cost me my job.

To add to it, there were such huge gray areas in the newfound theology, and gray scared me.

Gray meant I could get in trouble.

I enjoyed the black and white life of Evangelicalism because it was safer, even if it did sap my joy. I knew what to do, what not do, and everything in between. The way I was supposed to live was written out for me, and there wasn't much room to wiggle inside that. The Evangelical way is easy. You get your points with God. You don't have to struggle with theology much because it's already been struggled with for you. You just go to church and get told what to believe, and how to live. Then you just go do it.

As I continued, though, I knew that this was all changing.

It scared the hell out of me.

I think it scared our whole little group. Our Evangelical foundation was being uprooted right out from under us, and whenever you shake someone's foundation, it gets a little daunting for the individual. Whenever that begins to happen, you start to grasp for straws, only for those to be uprooted, too. It happens fast and leaves you waking up one day wondering what happened.

After a few months of meeting together, it got to the point that our weekly meetings turned into at least one person's saying, "I just don't know any more. I feel like I've been lied to. I feel like everything I've ever known was a lie. God is not who I've been taught He is."

The truth is, the Gospel has a way of rocking your world, turning it upside down, and leaving you breathless, not really knowing what's next. If it doesn't, then you probably haven't really dug into the Gospel of Jesus Christ.

This is just how God is, in my experience. He loves us, adores us, and actually likes us; but He is not scared to knock us off of our theological high horses, either. Because with God, theology is not the hill to die on; love is (1 Cor. 13:2).

As Rich Mullins liked to say, "God is like the kid who beats you up real bad, and then gives you a ride home on his bicycle." By this time, we had all been knocked down pretty brutally by Christ, and we were praying for the moment God picked us back up.

This was a very exciting, but very frightening, time for me. There was one specific moment that I remember as the point of no return. It was when I realized that how I had approached the Bible was all wrong. This was a game changer.

I was reading *A New Kind of Christianity* by Brian McLaren, and he was explaining how people read Scripture. He proposed that there are two ways in which people read Scripture.

The first of these ways, the conservative way, is called a "constitutional" reading. This is where we treat Scripture like the Constitution, in which every single word, punctuation, and thought is the inspired, hand-scribed, word of God, meaning that it is the Law of God.

We don't ask questions.

We don't poke and prod.

We take it for what it says because it's God's Word.

This is the way I had always been taught to view Scripture. In my tradition, Scripture teeters on being a fourth person in the trinity, next to the Father, Son, and the Holy Spirit. So, this is the only way I ever knew how to read the Bible. I never even questioned this approach.

However, McLaren proposed a second way to read Scripture. This is what he calls the "inspired library" approach. McLaren says that Scripture truly is inspired by God, but in a different way. God collected the Scriptures, after men wrote them. Over the course of thousands of years, these various writers wrote the stories, the traditions, and the teachings that they had heard in their lives. They were writing letters to one another and conversing about who God is, what God expected, and their own experiences with God.

They were having a conversation about God.

The Spirit collected these writings, and these writings (the Bible) are given to us as a look back into the history of the conversation of God and compels us to continue this conversation that has been going on for thousands and thousands of years.

As our group read this, it really shook us to our core. Mainly because it made so much sense to all of us.

It made more sense than the constitutional style we had always known. It accounted for all of those contradictions we had swept under the rug for years. It called us to actually look at the context of what we were reading and to dig deeper into Scripture. The inspired library view of Scripture made us fall in love with Scripture for what it is, and made us want to know more about it.

We would talk for hours on end about what this meant for us, and we all realized one thing: it meant a complete revamping of our faith.

This didn't mean that we lost our faith. I can only speak for myself, but it made my faith go even deeper. It opened up a whole new mystery to who God is, his intervention with mankind, and what this meant for us. It made me want to learn more. So that is what I did.

Chapter Twelve

If it was true that Scripture was an inspired library, what did this mean about those verses that had to do with homosexuality? Was what I was taught all my life wrong? Or, at best, honestly mistaken and slightly off?

The big question for me was whether there were actual people —who were not gay— who believed homosexuality was not a sin? This addendum was very important to me. I had met gay people online who didn't believe it was a sin, but I had yet to meet a straight Christian who believed homosexuality was okay in God's eyes. I felt like I needed to hear it from a straight person because they had no dog in their fight. To hear it from them — someone who had nothing to gain by saying it — meant that they really believed it, and had reasons to believe it.

This is why straight allies are so important to the LGBTQ (Lesbian, Gay, Bisexual, Transgender, Queer) community — it is for those people who are still in the closet.

Whenever someone who is openly gay makes a statement toward the advancement of gay rights, others are able to assume that they are just getting what they want, and they're only saying it's moral because that's what they want to say to give in to their flesh. But when a straight ally comes along and says he or she is in support the LGBTQ community because of the personal belief that homo/bisexuality is not a sin, that person's assertion carries a little more weight. This isn't the straight person's fight. The very fact that straight people are willing to stand alongside their LGBTQ brothers and sisters says far more than they know.

I went searching to see if there really were straight Christians out there who believed, with sound Biblical evidence, that homosexuality was not a sin.

It was a Sunday morning, and Kehila, our secret Bible study community, had been meeting for about a year now. I had since graduated from college, and my church office had become my domain. It was a cold, January morning, and I had just finished opening ceremonies for Sunday school. I got all of the youth off to their respective classes, and I had an hour to kill before worship. I went to my office and began searching to see if these straight, Christian allies existed.

It didn't take me long. I immediately found a website for a group called the Outlaw Preachers. Across the top was a banner that read, "Tell me, you who want to live under the law, do you know what the law actually says? (Gal. 4:21, NLT)"

Well, they had used my favorite book of the Bible, and one of my favorite verses, so they definitely had my attention. I began to read what they were saying.

I read their statement of faith, their stance on different issues, and their views on grace and salvation.

These people had a lot of the same theology I did, but they took it even further.

All of the questions I always wanted to ask, they had already asked and worked hard to answer them.

I was captivated by everything they wrote.

Then, I saw it: it was link to an article about their view of homosexuality. The article talked about how they were affirming of homosexuals, believed God loved them just like anyone else, and were not calling them to change.

I didn't really know how to respond. It was a lot all at once. But the very fact that these straight people — many of them ministers — were saying these things struck such a deep chord within me. Their website led to a Twitter hashtag called outlawpreachers, so I instantly checked it out.

I perused the usernames to see who they were. I found ministers from all different sorts of denominations. I found people of all ethnicities, of all sexualities, and even a few atheists/agnostics.

I noticed one of them lived fairly close to me, and she seemed to be one of the leaders within this group, so I sent her a direct message on Twitter just as I slipped out of my office to the worship service.

———————

The worship service seemed to drone on forever. I couldn't quit thinking about that website. I was really antsy, hoping for a quick response from her. The service finally ended, and I hurried to check my messages.

Nothing.

I went home and waited.

Nothing.

The next morning I woke up, and the first thing I did was check my messages.

Nothing.

I waited.

I was wanting so badly just to talk to someone from this newfound group of believers I could hardly stand the anticipation.

Finally, that Monday afternoon, I received a message back via Twitter that said she would love to talk to me more. Her name was Connie Waters, and she lived in Memphis, which was only about an hour and a half away. Fortunately for me, I was in seminary in Memphis at the time, so I traveled over there once a week anyway. We planned to meet that week before I went to class and chat.

I was thrilled. I was going to meet my first straight ally.

———————————

That Thursday, I left for seminary a couple of hours early, and met Connie at Chick-fil-A, just up the road from where I went to class. She pulled up in the parking lot and stepped out of the car, smiling. I had never once in my life talked to a female preacher nor a straight ally. I didn't know what to expect, or even what to call her, for that matter. So, I settled for just calling her Mrs. Connie.

If there was one thing she wasn't though, it was formal.

She was so joyful, it was infecting.

We ordered our chicken sandwiches and started chatting. I think she could tell I was semi-uncomfortable. Although, it wasn't so much that I was uncomfortable; I was more anxious. There was so much I wanted to say to her, but I just didn't have the courage. I wanted to tell her I was gay. I wanted to hear her say that it was okay. I wanted her to tell me that God loved me anyway. I had missed my chance with Mrs. Lopez, and I really didn't want to miss it again.

Instead, we talked about theology and how much mine had transformed over the last couple of years. She told me her story about leaving the Methodist church, and I could tell she had scars of her own. But we bonded over those scars.

Almost instantly, we became good friends.

I did poke and prod with questions, though. Even though I wasn't going to tell her outright about myself, I was going to pick her brain. I finally asked her, "What are your thoughts on homosexuality?"

She smiled. I could tell she was weighing me just as much as I was weighing her. I mean, here was this young Baptist minister sitting across from her, and she wasn't sure if she could trust me or not. I could see it in her eyes that she had fought this debate one too many times, and she was too tired to fight it again. I knew she was going to give me straightforward answers, but she was not about to argue, either.

She simply replied, "I believe every human being is a child of God and deserving of love."

It was so simple, yet so profound. However, it resonated with all that I had been learning over the past couple of years.

It made sense. Because of Christ, we are all free from the law and all brought into the fold of God's kingdom. God loves us. Period.

No addendums. No questions. No condemnation.

God just simply loves us.

We are His.

I don't think I held back my smile well enough. I didn't want to give too much away, but I was excited. I had heard it from a straight person's mouth. It was a big moment for me.

We wrapped up the meeting and exchanged phone numbers. I could tell we were going to be friends for a really long time, and I was as happy as I had been in a long time. I left there and went on to seminary, but I don't think I heard a thing the professor said that night. I simply wanted to read more about all these things Connie was telling me.

Chapter Thirteen

I got home around midnight from school. My roommate was asleep and so I just went to my bedroom. I put my backpack down beside my bed, and knelt beside my bed.

I prayed.

I prayed hard.

God, I know You love me. I have begun to realize that. And I thank You so much for loving me just as I am. But I'm also confused, God. I don't know who or what to believe. Both sides are telling me such conflicting stories, but both sides have evidence, too. You know I am attracted to men. You know I always have been. But, I don't want to act on my attraction if it's against You, either. I am okay with spending my life alone if that's how it's supposed to be. But if that's not what You're asking of me, I want to have companionship, as well.

So, God, I'm going to do the thing that I've been holding off on doing for a really long time. I'm going to look into what people say in favor of homosexuality. I always told myself never to read it because it would deceive me. But, now I don't think that's the case. I've learned that You aren't scared of our questions. So, Father, I pray that You guide me. I give this to You. Either way it turns out, I will be okay. Just give me some clarity. I need You right now, God.

Straight-Face would never let me research into the topic of homosexuality. I had tried to read into it before, but he always shut it down before I could go any further. He was scared that what I would read would convince me, and at the time, I really didn't want to be convinced. I was too scared that they would be right.

But now, it was time to stop putting off reading into this for myself.

I got up and grabbed my laptop out of my backpack, and I opened up Google. I began reading the arguments in favor of homosexuality's not being a sin.

That night I started an adventure that was going to take me months to work through. I began to open up my mind in ways I never had before, and was asking questions I had always wanted to ask. After it was all said and done, what I learned changed everything. I had no idea some of these arguments went so deep.

The first thing I found was that there were only seven verses in the entire Bible that relate to homosexuality in some way. These verses are usually deemed "clobber verses" because of the way religious people use these verses to clobber the arguments that say homosexuality is not a sin. I had formulated a plan that I was going to study each passage individually and dig through each of them until I couldn't dig anymore. I didn't care how long it was going to take me. I was determined.

---

1. Sodom and Gomorrah - Genesis 19:1-11

I was very familiar with this passage of Scripture because it is frequently preached within Evangelical Christianity.

The way the story was taught to me all of my life is that Lot and his family were staying in the city of Sodom when two angels, purportedly appearing as two human men, came to visit them. The two angels were given a place to stay in Lot's house, and all was going well. That is, until that night. All of the men from the town gathered around Lot's house and began demanding that Lot give them the two men so that they could rape them in the streets. Not wanting to give these two men over to these homosexual, sex-hungry mobsters, Lot instead offered his two virgin daughters instead. But, the angels, disgusted with the amount of homosexuality in this town, saves Lot and his family by sending them out of the town, and then God rains down burning sulfur from the sky. The town was destroyed, and poor Lot's wife was turned into a pillar of salt because she looked back.

As it was preached to me, it was clearly stated in black and white just what God thought about homosexuality. If you were a homosexual, then you might as well be prepared for burning sulfur from the sky. But, as I studied these verses, I realized how much of a leap that is for this passage. I never questioned it before because, well, that was frowned upon.

This is not a valid passage to call a monogamous, committed relationship between two individuals of the same sex a sin. The problem in this passage is the lack of concern for human dignity. The people in the town were going to commit awful acts to these two angels just because they wanted to.

It was not consensual.

It was not in love.

It was nothing but vile, putrid evil.

Take this modern fictional story as an example:

In the movie *Deliverance*, a group of men decide to canoe a river that was about to be dammed up because it would be the last time they would have the chance to do so. They set out on the river, into the forest of the deep south. While on their trip, they stop to rest, and then are attacked by some of the locals. These snaggle-toothed rednecks rape two of the men. They hold them down, against their will, and perform sexual acts on them. One of them, the character played by Ned Beatty, is anally raped while his other friend is held at gunpoint on his knees. Just as the other guy was about to be forced to perform oral sex, their other two friends save them.

No one in his right mind would honestly compare this scenario with that of two men or two women who love one another and are in a consensual, monogamous relationship. The analogy just doesn't work, in the same way you wouldn't compare a man raping a woman with that of a man and woman having consensual sex in their relationship.

The story of Sodom and Gomorrah is not about homosexuality by today's terms, no matter how you look at it. It's about rape.

As Rt. Rev. V. Gene Robinson once put it, "The story is about homosexual rape - and like any rape, it is an act of violence, not an act of sexuality."

What I found out next, though, is when I felt betrayed by my upbringing. Like I stated before, I had always been taught only one version of this story and never anything else. However, I was quite upset to find out that there are other places in Scripture that actually give commentary to this passage. But, these parts were never preached simply because it goes against the conservative view of the story.

Take the book of Ezekiel, for example. In chapter 16, verses 49-50 it states: "This was the guilt of your sister Sodom: she and her daughters had pride, excess of food, and prosperous ease, but did not aid the poor and needy. They were haughty, and did abominable things before me; therefore I removed them when I saw it." (NRSV)

The writer explains that the sin of Sodom was its pride, arrogance, inhospitality, and not taking care of the poor. As soon as I read this verse, I was angry. Here I was, just beginning my quest, and already I felt double-crossed by those from whom I had learned my theology. Surely, at least some of them had read these passages before and knew.

This seems to be the consensus throughout Scripture, as well. The writer of Hebrews (whom some believe to be Paul) even alludes to this in chapter 13, verse 2: "Do not neglect to show hospitality to strangers, for by doing that some have entertained angels without knowing it." (NRSV)

Some people like to make the statement that Jesus, in Matthew and Luke, compares the sins of Sodom to not taking care of the poor, as well. Personally, I believe this, but I don't think there is enough evidence to support it, either.

There are also a couple of verses where the sins of Sodom are listed as sexual. However, this does not mean homosexuality.

In fact, Jude makes it seem like one of their major sins was that they wanted to have sex with angels. Verse 7 says, "as Sodom and Gomorrah, and the cities around them in a similar manner to these, having given themselves over to sexual immorality and gone after strange flesh, are set forth as an example, suffering the vengeance of eternal fire." (NKJV)

Many read this verse and automatically assume that "strange flesh" means going after same-sex individuals. The Greek words used here are *sarkos heteras,* and would more likely refer to the fact that the men were trying to rape the angels that had come to the town, and has nothing to do with their gender.

I think the most fair consensus of this passage of scripture is that the sin of Sodom is depravity in general: from not taking care of the poor, to the utter lack of human safety and concern, to the mob of people wanting to rape two visitors to the town. The people in the town did not understand the word "hospitality," and they had completely fallen away from God's original design of community, love, and mutual respect of human dignity.

One thing stands, though: this passage says absolutely nothing about monogamous, consensual relationships between same-sex individuals, no matter how you look at it.

---

2. The Levitical Law – Lev. 18:22 and 20:13

If you are familiar with the arguments against homosexuality, you are probably more familiar with these two verses than any other verse in the Bible. It is from these verses that you hear that "homosexuality is an abomination." I decided to dissect these verses and get to the bottom of it.

If anywhere in Scripture it should be clear that homosexuality is a sin, it should be right here. I thought, "How could someone like Connie read these verses and still think it was okay?"

As she kept telling me during my studies, though: "Keep digging."

So I did.

First of all, I wanted to figure out what "abomination" really meant.

The Hebrew word that is often translated as abomination is *to'ebah*. It appears more than one hundred times in the Old Testament, and twenty-six of these times are in the Torah (the first five book of the Bible, in which the "Holiness Code" is found).

To'ebah means breaking a ritual law, doing something idolatrous, or that doing a certain act will make one unclean. In no way does it mean sin. The Hebrews had a word for sin: *zimah*. *To'ebah* was usually associated with an act that was pagan in nature and can be viewed as a way of saying, "We don't do that."

Once I began to read what else was an abomination to God, though, everything began to unravel.

According to Leviticus 11:10, it is an abomination to eat lobster and shrimp; and according to Deuteronomy 22:5, it is an abomination every time a girl puts on her boyfriend's sweatshirt, or (as some speculate) it could mean it's an abomination for any woman to ever wear blue jeans.

The word for abomination in these last two verses is the same used for Leviticus 18:22, where it says, "You shall not lie with a male as with a woman, it is an abomination" (NRSV). It's used again in Leviticus 20:13 when it says, "If a man lies with a male as he lies with a woman, both of them have committed an abomination. They shall surely be put to death. Their blood shall be upon them" (NKLV).

At this point, I was confused.

Here it said that homosexuality was an abomination, but it also said my recent visit to Red Lobster was as well. So, I came to the conclusion either I ignore all of the laws, or I follow them all. But this is when what I had learned over the past couple of years came in to play. The New Testament is very clear that through Christ, we are free from the law, because the law is fulfilled in Christ. The law doesn't change; it's simply fulfilled so that we are released from the bondage of the law. Therefore, the Levitical law should have no bearing on us today.

Sadly, though, this is not enough for a lot of people. They like to respond with, "Yeah, but it's still in there that God doesn't like gays, and God doesn't change, so we know he still doesn't like it. It's still an abomination."

To this answer, I could say that since God doesn't change, then that shrimp po'boy they had for lunch is *to'ebah* as well. But instead, I take a different route: I like to point out that this verse, much like Sodom and Gomorrah, is not talking about monogamous, consensual relationships between gay people. It's something altogether different.

One thing I learned from Brian McLaren that I will always cherish is the importance of putting Scripture into context. I began to study about the history of the Israelites, and why this verse may have shown up. The answer I found was both interesting, and satisfying.

Traditionally, it is believed that Moses wrote the book of Leviticus. We know now that it was probably written by a number of people over many years, but still we hold that Moses played a major part in the book. Moses had just led the Israelites out of captivity in Egypt. While in Egypt, they were enslaved by the Pharaoh and were forced to live by certain customs while they were used as labor. This means that the Israelites were also exposed to the Egyptian's beliefs and practices, and it is quite probable that many Israelites began to blend certain elements into their own lives and practices.

As stated, *to'ebah* means that something is idolatrous or unclean, but the word has its origin in an Egyptian word which means "holy" or "sacred." The Hebrews adopted the word, and changed its meaning as a way to carry negative connotations to the things practiced by the

Gentiles (non-Hebrews). The word is almost always used in the Old Testament in reference to some sort of idol worship.

Chapter 18 of Leviticus opens up with this proclamation:

"Then the Lord spoke to Moses, saying, Speak to the children of Israel, and say to them: 'I am the Lord your God. According to the doings of the land of Egypt, where you dwelt, you shall not do; and according to the doings of the land of Canaan, where I am bringing you, you shall not do; nor shall you walk in their ordinances. You shall observe My judgments and keep My ordinances, to walk in them: I am the Lord your God. You shall therefore keep My statutes and My judgments, which if a man does, he shall live by them: I am the Lord.'" (Lev. 18:1-5, NKJV)

The entire context of Leviticus 18 is that the author is going to list practices of Egyptians and Canaanites, and that the Hebrews were to stay away from such practices. One of these practices that was quite common in Egypt was that of temple prostitution as a form of worship to a goddess. (These male prostitutes were called *kadesh*.) The word used in verse 22 for mankind is the Hebrew word *zakar*. This word was primarily used in association with a male priest or a man with a religious duty, and in this case, is used to refer to the male who is passive in a sexual relationship in the goddess worship. The Egyptian male priests would take the role of a woman in a sexual relationship as a way to worship their goddess. So, verse 22 becomes "You shall not lie with *zakar* as with a woman. It is *to'ebah*."

Long story short, it points to the fact that the Hebrews were not to take part in this form of worship because the worship of God is not done in this manner. The Hebrews were commanded not to take part in this pagan ritual and to stay away from this form of goddess worship that could have easily carried over from Egypt.

What we do know is that, just like with Sodom and Gomorrah, the Levitical Law says nothing about monogamous, committed relationships between two men or two women.

As I kept studying, the black-and-white areas were quickly turning to gray, and I was feeling more and more betrayed by what I had been taught all of my life. I wanted to press on. I wanted to learn more.

---

3. Approaching the New Testament and Jesus — Matt. 19:37- and Matt. 8:5-20

After reading through the Sodom and Gomorrah story, and studying up on the Levitical law, I was surprised to find out that these three passages are the only clobber verses there are to homosexuality in the Old Testament. This was it? I was expecting it to take a lot longer to get through the Old Testament references, but here I was already past it and into the New Testament.

One thing I found very interesting was that Jesus was completely silent on the issue. Not once did he ever say anything that even translates to "homosexual" in any variance of the term. I find this interesting, considering it is such a big deal today.

Why are Christians holding on to something so tightly that Jesus never even talked about?

I did find one thing Jesus said, though, that took me a while to process. I would spend days thinking about this passage, and how I should understand it. The passage comes from the Book of Matthew, and it goes as follows:

"And Pharisees came up to him and tested Him by asking, 'Is it lawful to divorce one's wife for any cause?' He answered, 'Have you not read that he who created them from the beginning made them male and female, and said, "Therefore a man shall leave his father and his mother and hold fast to his wife, and the two shall become one flesh"? So they are no longer two but one flesh. What therefore God has joined together, let not man separate.' They said to him, 'Why then did Moses command one to give a certificate of divorce and to send her away?'" (Matt. 19:3-7, ESV)

I have heard this passage preached in quite a few sermons at some of my old churches, and it was said that Jesus clearly defines marriage as being between a man and woman. It was usually linked with the creation story in Genesis, which meant therefore homosexuality is strictly against God's plan.

But, to come to that conclusion is a stretch. That is putting something into the Scripture that isn't there. When people make that conclusion, they are speaking for Christ by simply inferring what they think He would say about the issue, without having any evidence that this is what Jesus *would* say. This is a dangerous thing to do. No one wants to find out once it's too late that he or she have spoke out of line for Christ, and spoke something that wasn't true, to boot.

Yes, in this passage, Jesus is telling the Pharisees about marriage and divorce, but He is speaking in the context that they knew of marriage. Jesus says a couple of things in this passage. First, He says that in the beginning, God made them male and female. I don't think anyone disagrees with this.

Jesus does not follow this up by saying, "And these two were specifically made to be married to one another." If He said that, He would be contradicting something else that He said: some people were born eunuchs, some people chose to be eunuchs, and some people were made eunuchs (Matt. 19:12). Eunuchs were not to be married and they were to remain single their whole lives. They were not "made to be with a woman," as is asserted by many on the previous verses. They were simply created, and that's all we know from this specific verse that Jesus is saying: God made men and women.

Now, in the second part, Jesus says that a man shall leave his parents and take his wife, and the two shall become one flesh. Again, nobody disagrees with this. We see it happen every day, and all understand that some men marry some women, and it is good. He does not say that some men cannot be with some men, and some women cannot be with some women. That is the inference, and it is an unfair one to make when we know so little about what Jesus actually thought about it.

After weeks of thinking on this one, I finally came to the conclusion that we cannot make such a bold assumption and place it in the mouth of Jesus, because that is dangerous for more than one reason. Secondly, if it were such a big issue to Jesus, why would He not have plainly spoken about it? It's not like He didn't know about monogamous, committed relationships between the same-sex. It did happen in His time, especially under Roman culture.

Instead, He remains silent on the issue.

However, His silence may speak very loudly.

In Matthew 8, and also in Luke 7, we read the story of Jesus' healing the Roman centurion's slave boy. This passage may have some very important implications.

In ancient Rome, homosexuality was not unknown nor was it taboo. However, to be homosexual in ancient Rome did not mean that one did not marry. Women, much like everywhere else during this time, were seen as property; and especially in Rome, women were a means of advancing one's status in society. So, if a person were homosexual in ancient Rome, he still married just as anyone else.

Not unlike heterosexual Roman men, the homosexual Roman men would find their lovers not in their wives, but in others - usually servants. This Roman Centurion may, in fact, be one of these men.

The passage from Matthew goes as follows:

"When he entered Capernaum, a centurion came to him, appealing to him and saying, 'Lord, my servant is lying at home paralyzed, in terrible distress.' And he said to him, 'I will come and cure him.' The centurion answered, 'Lord, I am not worthy to have you come under my roof; but only speak the word, and my servant will be healed. For I also am a man under authority, with soldiers under me; and I say to one, "Go," and he goes, and to another, "Come," and he comes, and to my slave, "Do this," and the slave does it.' When Jesus heard him, he was amazed and said to those who followed him, 'Truly I tell you, in no one in Israel have I found such faith. I tell you, many will come from east and west and will eat with Abraham and Isaac and Jacob in the kingdom of heaven, while the heirs of the kingdom will be thrown into the outer darkness, where there will be weeping and gnashing of teeth.' And to the centurion Jesus said, 'Go; let it be done for you according to your faith.' And the servant was healed in that hour. (Matt. 8:5-20, NRSV)

The word that the centurion uses for his ordinary slaves that he commands around is *doulos*, which was the common Greek word for slave. However, when speaking of the boy who is sick, the centurion uses the word *pais*, which can also be translated as a servant that was the master's male lover. The centurion makes a distinction between this one servant and all of the rest. This servant he loves; he is special to the centurion. Why else would this proud Roman centurion ride all the way to find a poor, homeless Hebrew teacher, and ask him for help? It's because this centurion was desperate, and he wanted badly to save this *pais* whom he adored.

It is very likely that the centurion and the *pais* were lovers, and Jesus would have known this, as well, since He would have been aware of the common Roman practice. What is Jesus' response? Does He tell the Roman centurion that he is a sinner, and that he need to "go and sin no more?" Not at all. In fact, He turns to His own Hebrew disciples and says that this Roman centurion has more faith than anyone else Jesus has met in Israel. That is remarkable!

The story ends on a happy note as the Centurion goes home to find that the *pais* had been healed and will live another day.

As I learned this bit about Jesus, it made me excited to know what else the New Testament had in store.

---

4. Arsenokoites and Malakos –
1 Cor. 6:9-10 and 1 Tim 1:9-11

As I continued on my quest through the New Testament, I was surprised to find that every reference that can be linked to homosexuality in the New Testament all came from Paul. A few people believe Jude speaks about homosexuality, but most scholars believe that Jude is talking about something totally different: humans having relations with angels, or "strange flesh." (Jude 1:7-8) There is not, by any means, enough evidence to link what Jude says to homosexuality.

The first two verses I went to were from two different letters of Paul: one to the Corinthians and one to Timothy. These two verses are familiar to most Evangelicals, as both of these passages are heard quite often. Most of the time, whenever the Levitical laws are taken out of the argument for whatever reason, the opponents of homosexuality will come back with these two verses:

"Or do you not know that wrongdoers will not inherit the kingdom of God? Do not be deceived: Neither the sexually immoral nor idolaters nor adulterers nor men who have sex with men nor thieves nor the greedy nor drunkards nor slanderers nor swindlers will inherit the kingdom of God." (1 Cor. 6:9-10, NIV)

"We also know that law is made not for the righteous but for lawbreakers and rebels, the ungodly and sinful, the unholy and irreligious; for those who kill their fathers or mothers, for murderers, for adulterers and perverts, for slave traders and liars and perjurers—and for whatever else is contrary to the sound doctrine that conforms to the glorious gospel of the blessed God, which he entrusted to me." (1 Tim 1:9-11, NIV)

The First Corinthians passage was the most troubling for me. As I read it, I almost wanted to completely give up. I felt like this was more straight forward than the Leviticus verses; plus, it was the New Testament. Being in the New Testament meant that it was post-Jesus and could not be swept under the rug as being "part of the Old Testament so it didn't apply to me." To top it off, Paul was saying that "homosexual offenders" would not inherit the kingdom of God.

I did what I did before, and I started looking at the original words, and just as I assumed, things started getting murky.

One of the most interesting things that caught my attention as I started looking was that the word "homosexual" was a fairly new word. Homosexuality was a word coined by psychologists in 1892 to simply explain male-to-male relationships and attractions.

This led to a huge question: If that word hadn't even been invented until 1892, then is that the most proper translation from the original Greek?

Let me give a side note about translations. Translating the Bible from Greek or Hebrew to English is not as easy as finding the one word and replacing it with another. Languages do not work that easily. For every language, there are words that fall into different contexts, which can change the meanings of the words or phrases when translated from one language to another, especially when you begin to use figurative language.

For example, the Spanish have a word, *cariño*, which refers to a type of love that is different from a romantic love. It is the type of love one feels for a best friend or a close family member, but it is different from the type of love you would feel for a husband or wife. When used as a verb, it can also mean literally caressing someone. If it is used as a noun, it can mean a person who is loving, tender, or showing affection. There are variations of the word to mean different things, depending on how it is used. However, this word is not translatable to English. We have no counter-part word that we could just "plug-in" and use. Instead, if we were to translate it to English, we would have to explain the word, just as I did above.

When translating ancient Greek to English, it gets even tougher. Even using the same concept of "love," the English only have one word for it: love. Greeks, however, had five different words for love, and they all meant different types of love, each with their own connotation and denotation.

So, when studying the original Greek or Hebrew of any passage, it is difficult to determine exactly what the authors meant, and many times, the scholars and translators have to use their best guesses in deciding what the passage is actually saying.

After much reading and studying, I found that the words that some scholars translate as homosexuality from the original Greek were *malakos* and *arsenokoites*. *Malakos* was translated as "male prostitute," and *arsenokoites* was translated as "homosexual offenders". But, what I found interesting was that in the First Timothy passage (which is why I included it above), *arsenokoites* is translated as "perverts". That's a big difference. So, why the switch?

What I found out is that, in reality, scholars are not really sure about how to translate these two words. These words aren't very common in our understanding of ancient Greek, especially *arsenokoites*. There is a lot of inferring as to what Paul "probably meant." And, as we saw from the Matthew passage, inference can be dangerous and not very reliable.

For me, it wasn't enough and was, quite simply, unfair. I mean, the way I was going to spend the rest of my life – and possibly eternity – depended on what was being said here, and all I could find was "this is what Paul probably meant." It made me more than a little frustrated.

I found out that there is no consensus among Biblical scholars as to what is meant by these two words. *Malakos* is translated as pervert, effeminate, self-indulgent, and male prostitute. *Arsenokoites* is translated as homosexual offenders, perverts, men who practice homosexuality, and sexual perverts.

I didn't know a lot about Greek language and translations at the time, but I did know that generally, when translators cannot agree on the meaning of a Greek word, it showed what little they knew about the word.

The word *malakos* was better known than that of *arsenokoites*. *Malakos* is seen more often in Greek texts, and it literally means "soft". Sometimes, translators take this to mean effeminate men. I think you know as well as I do that there are some straight men out there who are far more effeminate than some gay men. So, if this is the meaning of the word, then homosexuals are not the only people who are in trouble.

There are also other times in Greek texts where *malakos* is translated as being reckless and uncontrolled in the way a person acts.

So, while we don't know the exact meaning of the word today, we do not have any evidence whatsoever that *malakos*, in the first-century when Paul was writing, meant homosexual men. *Arsenokoites* is a much more limited word because the translations are much closer in nature. But the problem with this word is that many scholars agree, and will admit, that this word is almost impossible to translate. Although *malakos* was more widely used, *arsenokoites* can be found in some other Greek works as well; seventy-three to be exact. In almost every other use of the word, even up to the sixth century, the word was used explicitly to talk about male slaves who were bought strictly for the purpose of sex. This was the moment things began to make sense. It also made sense when compared to the Levitical law and with the story of Sodom and Gomorrah. It seems more logical that in First Corinthians, Paul was actually saying neither male prostitute (*malakos*) nor male sex slave trader (*arsenokoites*) would inherit the kingdom of God. Again, this is not talking about monogamous, committed relationships. Paul is talking about people in the sex trade, both as a business and as related to male temple prostitution.

With this in mind, Scripture was starting to make sense in a whole different way. The Old Testament laws and the New Testament were beginning to intertwine in a new, fresh way. The angry, wrathful God I used to know was suddenly becoming an advocate for human dignity. All of these passages began to flow together throughout all of Scripture to show that all human beings were equal in status. We should live by one basic code: love.

It all started clicking after learning the meanings of these two words, and I was excited about how it was coming together. Scripture was making far more sense than it used to. It was becoming less of a manual of rules, and more of an ethical teaching about how to view others and love another.

As I learned these two words and their contexts, the anger at my upbringing was becoming excitement about where my life was going and the things I was learning.

But, I wasn't quite finished yet!

---

5. Romans 1

I had saved this passage for last, because this was the most widely used clobber passage in Scripture. I had heard this passage preached more than just a few times, and it was always the go-to verse in any debate about homosexuality and Christianity. The problem with this verse for the person trying to be an advocate for homosexuality is that this passage is clearly about same-sex relationships. There is just no way around that.

Whenever I had come to some amazing conclusion about the other verses, my mind would always wander back to this passage, because I was pretty sure there was no way around this one. Even though what I learned about the other passages made me excited, this passage was always my buzz-kill.

In Romans Chapter 1:26-27, Paul wrote:

"Because of this, God gave them over to shameful lusts. Even their women exchanged natural relations for unnatural ones. In the same way the men also abandoned natural relations with women and were inflamed with lust for one another. Men committed indecent acts with other men, and received in themselves the due penalty for their perversion." (NIV)

What's interesting, as a side note, is that this is only place in Scripture where lesbianism is brought into play. In all the other passages – literally every other one of them – the writer is talking about male-to-male relationships. This is the only place in the entire Bible that female-to-female relationships are even mentioned.

We never get a command that says women having sex with other women is an abomination, nor do we hear that lesbians will not inherit the kingdom of God. The only thing we derive, if we take this passage at face value, is that a woman having passions for another woman is simply lustful.

So, the question remains: What do we do with this passage? I mean, it's pretty straightforward, is it not?

Well, yes and no.

Paul makes it clear that something perverse is going on here, and he is not happy about it. But the more I read the commentary on this passage and dug around, the less I was convinced that it was entirely the sexual acts with which he was disgusted.

Just as with the other passages, whenever you put them in context, black and white suddenly becomes a little grayer. When you take a step back and read the verses before it, you can see a little more about what Paul is talking about:

"For although they knew God, they neither glorified him as God nor gave thanks to him, but their thinking became futile and their foolish hearts were darkened. Although they claimed to be wise, they became fools and exchanged the glory of the immortal God for images made to look like a mortal human being and birds and animals and reptiles. Therefore God gave them over in the sinful desires of their hearts to sexual impurity for the degrading of their bodies with one another. They exchanged the truth about God for a lie, and worshiped and served created things rather than the Creator—who is forever praised. Amen.

Because of this, God gave them over to shameful lusts. Even their women exchanged natural sexual relations for unnatural ones. In the same way the men also abandoned natural relations with women and were inflamed with lust for one another. Men committed shameful acts with other men, and received in themselves the due penalty for their error." (Rom. 1:21-27, NIV)

I decided to look into breaking this passage down step by step and then learn some history behind it.

Before I began, I wanted to make sure I knew exactly who Paul was talking to in this letter. By the language he uses, and the context of the entire letter, we know that Paul is talking to the Jewish people who had been residing in Rome. From much of the rest of the letter, we know that the Jewish people that had been living there had given up much of their Jewish roots to begin serving the pagan gods of Rome.

So, this letter was written to the Jewish people of Rome because Paul had lumped them in with the Gentiles whom he was trying to reach with the Gospel of Jesus Christ (Rom. 1:6).

So first off, Paul says that the Jews in Rome knew God, but they didn't glorify Him, nor did they give thanks to Him anymore. According to Paul, this was their first mistake, because then they became futile in their thinking, and their hearts were darkened. For Paul, the problem all started with ignoring God. But it got worse!

They began to call themselves wise, but they were becoming fools. Why did they become fools? Because they exchanged the true, living God for idols that looked like human beings, birds, animals, and reptiles. Here, Paul is talking about Roman idol worship, which could be a pretty perverse thing.

He goes on to say that because of their idol worship, God gave them over to sexual impurity for the degrading of their bodies with one another. And as we know from what Paul says in First Corinthians 6, when we have sex and it is not in pure, monogamous, committed relationships, then we are degrading our bodies because our bodies are temples of the Holy Spirit.

God has designed sex for intimacy between two people who have committed themselves to one another to be as one. So, anything outside those boundaries of sex is harmful to us because it goes against what God has intended. Therefore, it is degrading to our own bodies. Now, there is much room to believe that Paul is talking about all sexual impurity here – both homosexual and heterosexual – because in the next line, he goes back to the former thought, therefore starting a whole new train of thought.

Paul is simply making a statement that says: "sexual impurity of any kind is harmful, and the type of which I am talking is happening because of the way these people ignored God and started worshipping idols."

In the next line, Paul begins a new train of thought by going back a step. Again, he reiterates that these people exchanged truth for a lie, and began to worship created things instead of the Creator himself. Because of this, Paul says that God gave them over to shameful lusts, and that their women began exchanging natural relations for unnatural ones, and the men followed suit.

I must point out what "natural" means when Paul says that word. In today's language, we think of natural as what nature has intended, therefore meaning "what God intended."

But, this isn't the case for when Paul was writing.

When someone in Paul's time used the word "natural" in their writings, they were more closely talking about what is cultural and what is taboo. So, when Paul is talking about what is "natural," he is speaking about what is common among his people group, and when he says "unnatural," he is speaking about what is taboo among this same group. Paul is not making a blanket theological statement here that says that because God designed them male and female, then it is "unnatural" for two of the same kind to be together. A lot of readers assume this, though, and that is an inferred proposition that leads us into the same paths we always took.

For instance, if it were "unnatural" for two of the same gender to be together, then we would attribute this to humanity's free will. In other words, God designed it one way, but because of human depravity, we have rebelled against God's design and have done it our own way.

However, this argument falls apart when you look outside of humanity and start researching the animal kingdom, in which I believe most would agree that they do not have the same level of free will that humans have. But, you may be surprised to find that homosexuality has been found to occur in fifteen hundred animal species. The number is believed to be much higher, but those are just the ones scientists have found. Homosexuality occurs in everything from crabs to dolphins to lions to dwarf chimpanzees, which are the closest relatives to human beings in the animal kingdom. As a consensus, scientists are pretty certain that homosexuality is anything but *unnatural* in this world. In fact, some researchers and professors, such as Peter Boeckman of the University of Oslo, even claim that it has been essential to the lives of some species.

So, what exactly is Paul talking about here?

Well, since we know that the context is Roman idol worship, let's take a look at their religious practices.

Roman people were serving a Syrian goddess named Cybele. The idol god Cybele was transported to Rome around 204 BC, where she was greeted with glee. The Roman people quickly assimilated their culture to this new god they called the Great Mother of Rome. They considered her the god of other gods, of beasts, and of human beings. She was also seen as being both male and female, even though her female characteristic is what was more honored.

Cybele's lover, Attis, was said to have emasculated himself and bled to death under a pine tree. To commemorate this, the male priests of Cybele would mourn his death by re-enacting the castration. They would take sharp stones and emasculate themselves (which sounds horrid) and then dress in women's clothing. Their worship was usually marked with these practices, and these new "women" would have sex with the men. The worship of Cybele was marked by wild orgies where men would sleep with men, and women would sleep with women. There is also some evidence that worship of Cybele involved human sacrifice and cannibalism.

Following from this, it's no doubt that Paul had some problems with the Jewish people's getting caught up in these wicked pagan practices. The Jews were supposed to be the people who were seen as God's holy and set apart people. Paul was not happy with the fact that certain Jewish people were taking part in this type of worship. This is why in Romans 2:1, he really drives home his point when he tells them that when they judge these Cybele worshippers, they are judging themselves, because they are doing the same thing.

Romans 1 quickly began to unravel as all of this soaked in. Paul didn't want them to get caught up in the pagan world, because it would drive them away from the true, living God. It was never about same-sex relationships; it was always about wild, sexual, idol worship.

6. Taking it all in

And that's it. No, really. Those are all of the verses in the entire Bible that had to do with homosexuality.

Everything I had ever been taught about these passages was false whenever I decided to look into each passage for myself and study the history, context, and more. Not once in scripture does it talk about homosexuality in the way we know it today.

Every time a reference was made in scripture, it had to do with human dignity, slavery, the sex trade, or idol worship. All of these things are seen as sinful in heterosexuality, as well.

Nothing is said about attraction.

Nothing is said about committed relationships.

Nothing is said about being in love.

The only laws and rules made were simply to protect humans and help us to love one another, which is directly in tune with the rest of Scripture.

It took me a few months to really study all of this, and by the time I finished, I was approaching another summer in youth ministry. But, I had a sense that things were going to be really different.

Chapter Fourteen

I would like to say all of my confusion was out the window, but that wasn't the case at all. I still had Straight-Face, and he wasn't about to go away any time soon.

I had come to see that all of the theological arguments against homosexuality were gone, but it was still a huge step to say, "I believe it."

I knew that deep down I was becoming, or had already become, comfortable with believing that homosexuality inside a monogamous, committed relationship was not a sin. But I was still a youth minister at a very conservative Southern Baptist church in the buckle of the Bible belt. There was no way I could just one day say, "Oh, hey kids, I think being gay is okay. And by the way, I'm gay, too!"

I just couldn't imagine that would have gone over very well.

After much debate with myself, I got the courage to begin to bring these topics up to Kehila.

I presented them with all of the clobber verses and awaited their responses. The moment of silence after the presentation seemed like forever.

"Wow," said one of my close friends, Jimmy.

"So, what do you think?" I asked, nervously.

"I feel like I've been lied to is what I think," he replied.

"Really?" I asked, as I sighed a sigh of relief.

"Yeah, I agree," chimed in another friend of mine. He had a brother who was also gay, so I knew this had been something he had thought about before. He continued, "It just seems like we've all been taught one cherry-picking verse and have never been taught the rest of the story."

The rest of the group chimed in much of the same way. They were looking at the evidence and were progressing in their theology in much the same way I had been, and we were continuing to grow as a community. I had become quite proud to call this group my community, and we were getting closer every week.

At the same time, though, we were becoming more and more hidden about our group because the stakes were growing much higher. They understood that my job would be on the line if word got out about what we were discussing, so our group became tighter, and we began really caring for each other, watching each other's back.

We knew that over the course of the last two years, we had suddenly become progressive together, but almost all of us were somehow stuck within our conservative church – whether it was because of jobs or family ties. Our time together was simply a chance for everyone to breathe and take off their own respective mask's.

If there is one thing I learned from being in true community with other people is that we all have masks. Straight-Face was only one of many. Some people wear a mask to hide their porn addiction; others to hide their alcoholism. Some wear a mask to hide the shame of failure; others because they're too afraid to face the reality of the decisions they have made. Some people have a mask to cover up their pain, because they feel as if they must have it all together; others have a mask to cover up their fear, because they feel as if they must look courageous. All of us puts our masks on so that others can't see our true faces. But, ultimately, we all wear our masks so that we can hide from ourselves.

It's much easier to hide behind our masks and not admit the things about us that we don't want to be true. Instead, we just pretend those areas don't exist, and we move on in life, only for those parts to pop up when we least want them to. The bad thing about a mask is that, while it comforts us temporarily, it's weak against reality. Ultimately, reality always seeps in and reminds us that who we think we are is really just a mask pretending to be that person. Our true selves always spill out eventually. It's up to us whether we want to face our true selves head on and get it over with, or keep repressing it only to face it later.

At this point, I decided to do more repressing. I was more real with this group than I had ever been with any people in my entire life, but I still wasn't ready to fully take Straight-Face off. I still wanted them to believe I was straight. I didn't want to be that real with them, just in case one of them let it slip.

But, really, I began to think I was just being a coward. I didn't want people to see the real me, because at the end of the day, I was still ashamed of it. On top of that, I didn't want to be different from every one else. I was also scared it would change some of my friendships with these people.

It's one thing to be theologically okay with homosexuality; it's another thing to hang out with a homosexual. I didn't want there to be any uneasiness around me. I didn't want my own sexuality to degrade the message of grace. I was afraid that if they knew I was attracted to men, then everything we had learned about grace and Scripture would be forgotten, and they would assume I was just making stuff up to make it fit with what I wanted, which was a common argument I have heard from conservatives.

To be honest, though, a large part of me didn't want to be okay with homosexuality theologically. A lot of people today assume what I said before: that I just believe what I want to believe.

But the opposite is true, actually.

Life would have been a lot easier for me had I, through my studying, come to the conclusion that the conservative view was right, and that homosexuality was a sin. I had an amazing job and had such a wonderful youth group. Life is just easier as a conservative. Most things are black and white, and there's not much room for mystery or questions. You do what you're supposed to do, whenever you're supposed to do it, and you go on about your life. Plain and simple.

This is why one of the biggest pet peeves of most homosexuals is when they hear someone say that it's a choice. About 99 percent of all homosexuals would say they would never choose to be gay. Even if they embrace their sexuality and love who they are - much like I do today, at the end of the day, they know it would just simply be easier as a straight person. Nobody wants to choose to be hated, or outcasted, or unloved. Being gay carries baggage with it that straight people will never fully understand.

It's the same way that African-Americans would have been in the 1800s. They may have loved who they were, and they probably embraced their culture and their roots; but, they knew life would just simply be easier if they were white during that time. The whole argument of "choice" is simply asinine.

But either way, I didn't want myself, or my sexuality, to get in the way of the message, so I kept clinging to Straight-Face.

I could tell he was getting shaky, though.

He didn't like where things had taken me lately, and he was losing power. I was spending way more time with Straight-Face off than I was with him on, and I think I was starting to realize that, which made me even more apprehensive.

I was scared I was becoming so comfortable with myself that I was going to start letting on to who I really was, and when you're teetering that line, life can become tedious. I felt like I was always on a ledge, on the brink of falling off. I was jittery, never at ease. I was having anxiety attacks quite often, and stress was taking its toll on me like never before.

As summer of 2011 approached, I decided to set all of my attention on the ministry and stopped focusing on the theology so much. I knew I had to either be all in or all out. No matter what I believed about homosexuality or grace or the message, I had to decide what I was going to do about it in my own life. I weighed my options, and decided it best if I didn't tell anyone about my attractions. I decided it would be best if I continued living my life as a straight man, for the greater good.

For the greater good.

That's what I kept telling myself.

I have to think about the ministry. I have to think about the kids. I have to think about the church. I have to think about my parents. I have to think about my calling. I must live for other people — God's people.

This became my mantra.

For the greater good.

I recited it in my head in the mornings. I based most of my decisions on it. Even though I hadn't told Connie about my own attractions, I came to her with this idea. I told her where I was theologically, but that I wanted to stay within my own conservative church. I told her it was for the greater good. She didn't really give me an opinion either way. She just simply supported. She was good at doing that.

All of my attention went to playing this out. I started polishing off the old mask and getting back to work.

Just as summer neared, something happened though, and it threw me off a little bit. A former youth that was now in the college-ministry, who I talked to quite often, told me she was attracted to me and wanted to date.

I had never really dated much before. I had a couple of girlfriends throughout college. Mostly flings and nothing more. The most I had ever even done was kiss them. I really had no interest in sex with women whatsoever. I only dated because it was what I was supposed to do, and I was hoping that maybe I could force myself into liking women.

It never worked, but I thought if ever there was a girl who would make that happen, it would be this one. She was beautiful, smart, funny, had a heart for God and for mission work, and we could talk for hours about theology and grace and love and everything in between.

After some thought, I went to my pastor and told him about the situation. Because she was a former youth and still in the college ministry, it was a delicate situation, but he gave his blessing, considering I was only a few years older than she. So, I went for it.

We started dating right at the beginning of summer, and it was awkward, to say the least. Not that there was anything wrong with her. She was perfect. It was just awkward because I was trying to force it.

I was throwing out every Hollywood style dating cliché there was. I wanted so badly to love her. I wanted so much just to be completely attracted to her and be head over heels for her.

But the chemistry just wasn't there.

My doubts about the sinfulness of homosexuality even exacerbated the situation. I was on the brink of the biggest shift in my belief system as of yet, and here I was still trying so desperately to be a straight man. I think that's why I went for it, though. I knew that I was on the brink of accepting my own sexuality, so I had to give it one last big ditch effort.

I knew from the outset that this was probably not going to work, but I was going to give it everything I had to love this girl. I genuinely did love her, too, just not in an eros love. I loved who she was, and I loved the thought of being in love with her. But at the end of the day, I couldn't make that cross over into a deeper love like I knew I could probably have with a guy.

I knew it was pointless, but I kept trying anyways. I watched my brother marry, have a child, and be with a girl for a long span of time, and it didn't change the way he felt. One of my best friend's dad's had done the same thing, and it didn't change his attraction. I had heard story after story of married men coming out years, sometimes decades, later. I knew that no matter how far I took this thing, it wasn't going to change the way I felt.

However, I can be stubborn, and I was holding on to that one chance that maybe it would be different for me.

I settled in to the hot, summer youth ministry months. I would spend my days working at the church, my afternoons with my girlfriend and friends and sometimes students, and my nights talking with gay friends online. I was actually talking theology with them now, and was helping some of them with their own religious thoughts and depressions. It was nice to actually be using some of this information for good.

By this time, I had made a friend from California named Tyson who I talked to almost daily. I would seclude myself in the bedroom, so that my roommate and his girlfriend couldn't hear me, and Tyson and I would talk about life. He was in a similar situation, with a heavily Catholic family, and he couldn't figure out what he believed about his own sexuality, either. We were able to explore Scripture together and at least have that little window of time every day that we wouldn't have to wear our masks.

The summer was long, and often times difficult. I knew things had changed, but I didn't want to acknowledge it. My life was too comfortable, in the sense that this was what I always knew, and I was too scared of change.

Luckily, whenever we get too comfortable, God changes things even though we don't want it to.

Chapter Fifteen

Summer came to an end, and my routine continued. My students were back in school, and I didn't see my girlfriend as much because she was also on the college campus and too busy with school. Everything continued as normal until God took it upon himself to change things.

I was flipping through the daily news while sitting in my church office and up popped a news story about a fifteen-year old boy who hanged himself in his bedroom. He was a good-looking kid who smiled happily in the photo that was shown on the news piece. The kid was a good student and never got into trouble.

But, he was gay.

Because of this, he couldn't get past the deep sadness and guilt that came with his religious upbringing.

I had read articles and had seen news stories like this one before, but this particular one struck a nerve with me unlike any of them before. While I was reading, all of my past came screaming back at me. I thought about my own suicide attempts, and all the nights I lay in bed and thought about doing the same thing.

I wondered if this kid was bullied.

I wondered if anyone ever even knew what he was going through.

I wondered if he had a mask that taunted him like mine taunted me.

I wondered what went through his mind in those last moments.

And I wondered what his life would have been like had he lived.

I turned the television off and went about the rest of my day, but I couldn't shake this kid from my thoughts. I didn't even remember the kid's name, but his picture – that smile, that black hair, and those dark eyes – kept popping up in my head. I couldn't escape it.

All day long I thought about this kid, and it was keeping me from doing any productive work. I left my office at the church and went back home to an empty apartment. I didn't know where my roommate was, but I was glad he wasn't home. I jumped in the shower, hoping a nice warm shower would help me relax and ease the malaise.

It didn't work, though.

I just stood in the scalding hot water. As I kept thinking about the boy, and my own past, I couldn't help but become overtaken with emotion.

I began praying for peace in this boy's family, and that God use this situation to help other gay teenagers who were feeling the same depression in their own lives.

That was when, out of nowhere, God spoke to me as clearly as He had ever spoken to me before.

He simply said, "I want you to come out of the closet."

I stopped and stared at the wall of my beige shower. The tears stopped flowing and I just stood there, reeling in what I had just experienced.

Audibly, I replied, "Hell no!"

I went back to washing up, trying to ignore what I felt God had said to me, but eventually I tried to reason with God and myself.

Why would I do that? I have such a great thing going here. I have a great ministry, a lot of amazing kids. I just settled into this apartment, and what would my roommate think? No, no... what would my girlfriend think? My church would hate me. Even my own youth, some of them would probably hate me. I would lose my job. God, why would You ask me to do that? What about my dad? This could crush him. I don't understand.

God replied once again, to my surprise. I felt Him simply say, "Brandon, if you don't stand up and speak truth, you are part of the problem. This kid's blood, and the blood of others, will be as much upon your hands as anyone else's."

I was stunned. That was definitely not what I wanted to hear, which made my stubborn side angry.

Why are You trying to ruin my life, God? Why are You trying to mess this up? I have worked so hard at being who I always thought You wanted me to be, and what others have wanted me to be. I have worked so much, and I have been faithful in telling people about grace and love and Jesus Christ. I have done nothing but sacrifice. Why is that not enough? Why must You call me to do the one thing I have always asked that You not ask me to do? I don't understand!

But God didn't answer.

I'm pretty sure I sounded like a whiny teenager whose mom tells him that he's grounded. God remained silent, allowing me to smolder on His clear instructions.

I wasn't having it, though.

I told Him no and I was going to stick by it. I had already given

God so much, why couldn't He just budge on this? I was going to try and force His hand on this one and do it my way.

We all know how well that usually works out.

It became a daily fight for me from that point on. Every time I went to pray or read Scripture or do my daily office, God was there, reminding me of what He wanted from me, and that's all I was getting from him.

"I want you to come out," He'd say over and over again to me. It was starting to consume me, and nobody had a clue. I went about life, business as usual. I guess that's the great thing about Straight-Face: no matter how ugly and messed up the real you is, he just keeps smiling like nothing is wrong.

But Straight-Face and I were fighting a new fight now. Before, it was Straight-Face and God versus my homosexual desires. Now, like a twist in a wrestling tag team main event, everything flip-flopped and now it was Straight-Face and me versus what God wanted. I spent so long trying to hide that I was gay because I didn't think God would like that I owned up to it. Now, I was trying to hide that I was gay in spite of what I felt God was telling me.

Shortly into September, it began taking its toll on my relationship with my girlfriend. Straight-Face was telling me that I had to keep this relationship because it was my only link to sanity and normalcy, but I already knew that it was over. We were texting one night after not speaking with each other for a couple of days, and I think we both knew we were forcing it. I was driving back home and finally, I asked, "Are we kidding ourselves here?"

She responded, "I think so."

And just like that, it was over.

I passed my apartment and just kept driving. I didn't want to go inside. I didn't want to do anything, really. I just started crying as I was driving.

I wasn't crying over the relationship. I knew that was over a long time ago. I loved her for who she was, and I still care for her today. But I wasn't *in* love with her.

I was crying because I knew God was backing me into a corner, and my resistance was doing nothing but making things worse. My last ditch effort in trying to be a straight man had failed miserably, and I knew that the longer I carried on this game, the harder the fight was going to become.

Jesus was calling me out, much like He called his disciples.

He was asking me to leave what I knew.

He was asking me to leave comfort and security and to step out on faith into a great unknown.

He was asking me to jump off the edge of the cliff without even looking over the side first.

Just a blind jump.

He was asking me to be courageous.

But I was too big of a coward.

Thank God that when we don't always jump out in faith, He sometimes pushes us over the ledge for our own good.

The next week, my friend Jimmy and I were in a car headed to Nashville for the Outlaw Preacher Reunion. Since I first discovered the Outlaw Preachers (The OP's) on Twitter, Jimmy and some others from Kehila had jumped on board, and we had all become friends with many of the people in the group. The OP's decided that they were going to get everyone together for a weekend conference so that we could all talk and learn from each other. I was in the middle of my solitary crisis, and

I knew that I needed to escape Jonesboro, even if just for a weekend. I proposed to Jimmy that we go to the conference, and he was on board. I couldn't exactly tell the people from my church that we were going to the Outlaw Preachers' conference. Some of the other pastors on staff had heard of the OPs before, and they were no fans of the group, to say the least. So, I kept my vacation's destination to myself, and I just simply called it a "Nashville trip."

Connie was there, as well as all of the others that we had come to know and love over the past year. The weekend was great, but it was anything but a vacation from my soul crisis. If anything, it intensified everything. Spending a weekend with a group of Christians who were affirming made me more confused about my own stance. These people were intensely spiritual, and at the same time, intensely real. They didn't seem to wear many masks. They didn't cover up their downfalls or try to play like they were perfect. They had faults, they had scars, and they didn't care if you saw them.

The reality that life after coming out was possible had, for the first time, entered my mind. Mind you, it didn't mean I was ready to pull that trigger, but it at least let me know that it was something that was plausible.

The next week after the conference, I was driving back to seminary for class, and had to face the hour-and-a-half drive there and back.

I had a lot on my mind.

Too much, really.

My parents, after a rocky year, had decided to get a divorce, and for much of the time I was playing the middle-man between the two of them. The shock of God calling me out of the closet was still fresh upon my mind and I was still quite bitter about it. On top of that, the things I had learned and experienced from the Outlaw Preachers Reunion were all still fresh upon my mind.

God and I were having a conversation on the way to seminary that night, and I was trying to make sense of everything.

God, I don't get it. Life right now is hell. Nothing makes sense. I don't feel like I know anything anymore, and I feel like I'm being backed into a corner.

"You know what I've called you to do," seemed to be the only response I could get back. It was the same response I'd gotten from Him since He originally called me to come out.

Why? Why must that be the thing? Why can't I have a say in this?

It didn't take much to make me angry by now. I was still determined to fight it as hard as I could, because above all else, it was the one thing I never wanted anyone to know.

Finally, I felt as if God said, "I've told you for a month now what I want from you. I've told you continuously, and you keep ignoring me. You keep saying no. So, I'm moving ahead of you. You can fight this all you want, and do it your way. That's fine. But whenever you are ready to catch up to me, I'll be waiting."

It's hard for me to put into words what began running through my head during that moment. It was fear, uncertainty, shame, and guilt. It was as plain as when He called me to come out in the shower a month before. I knew it was God talking to me, but I didn't want it to be true.

The next moment, it was as if He simply moved His Spirit away from me. Now, I know God never truly left me, because He will never truly leave us nor forsake us, but I definitely felt like God took His hand off of me that day, and let me do things my own way. In an instant, my heart dropped and I felt crushed. I felt like my entire life had finally unravelled, and I was left out in the cold. He really did move forward, and He was not coming back. For once, He was letting me fall flat on my face and wasn't going to catch me until I decided to obey and do it His way.

I couldn't really pay attention during class that night. Nothing felt right.

From that point on, I could barely pray anymore.

I couldn't even really read Scripture and get anything out of it.

The old Christian worship music I used to sing and enjoy just became empty words. I felt like David when he wrote:

"My God, my God, why have you forsaken me? Why are you so far from saving me, so far from my cries of anguish? My God, I cry out by day, but you do not answer, by night, but I find no rest" (Psalm 22:1-2, NIV).

When I was finished with class that night, I didn't go home.

I drove around for hours, just running things through my head.

I only had one person I could call and talk to about this: Tyson, my friend from the Internet. He was the only person who knew me without Straight-Face, and I knew I needed to converse with another human being about what was going on with me. If I didn't, I was going to explode.

"I just don't know what to do," I told him on the phone, as I drove around town. "My last hope was having a girlfriend, but I failed at that, too. God keeps taking every lifeline away from me. My parents are splitting, so I've got no stability there anymore. My closest friends don't know the real me. My own church would kick me to the curb. I feel like if I keep fighting this, things are just going to get worse."

"You're insane," he replied, half-jokingly.

"Well, that wasn't comforting!" I slightly laughed back.

But, he was being genuine. He understood where I was at, because he was in a similar situation with his family.

"Brandon, you're much further than me in this. Hell, you're the one I come to with questions on this stuff. Now, I'm not the most spiritual person in the world, but I know I wouldn't want to be fighting against God on anything. You know you can't win from the outset."

As I talked to him, it dawned on me that I had more chemistry with this guy that I had never even met in real life than I ever did with any girl. I realized in that moment that I would never be able to be happy with a girl. Ever. It just wouldn't work. It was too unnatural for me. This thought was another nail in the coffin.

"Yeah," I sighed, "I know you're right. I just really don't want you to be right."

We finished the conversation, and I thanked him for listening to me. I hung up the phone and kept driving around. It was around 2 A.M, and I realized how much my emotions were turning to anger.

Deep anger.

Bitterness about the situation; about who I was.

Bitterness toward God.

I began to blame Him for every bit of it.

I was pissed.

I was pissed at God; I was pissed at what He had and hadn't done in my life.

I knew it was pointless to be pissed at God, but I was.

This wasn't fair.

I had done everything I could to make You happy, and You're just going to abandon me like this? You are going to just throw me out there that easy? And why would You lead me to such a position anyways? Why won't You just change my attraction? I mean, You are the Creator of the whole damn universe; it wouldn't be that hard for You, would it? So, why won't You?

The more I drove, the more bitter and angry I became.

I had had enough of everything. If God wanted me to do things my own way, then that's what I was going to do.

That's the mindset I was going to adopt. If God was going to be like this, then I was going to stop trying to please Him. I was going to live for me. Sure, I still believed in the basic teachings of Jesus Christ: love God, love people. But, at this point in time, it was the loving God that I wasn't too hip on.

I was on the road to rebellion against God, and for the first time in my life, I didn't care one bit.

That night, I went back to my apartment and I poured myself a big glass of vodka that I had kept for I don't know how long. I chugged it, and I called up Tyson again. He could tell I was spiraling down.

He even pointed it out to me.

But I didn't care.

I was done playing this game with God. If God was going to stop caring, then I was, too.

I chugged another glass of vodka and finally faded off to sleep.

Chapter Sixteen

The next morning, the headache was strong, but I didn't care. I just hopped in the shower and let the hot water run over my body.

My mind was a blank, and I liked it that way.

I was on my own.

Well, sort of. I still had Straight-Face, but that wasn't much comfort.

But things had changed with him, too. He no longer had control. By the end of this summer, I was no longer a slave to him; he was a slave to me. I had him on when I needed him, but any other time, he was gone. Really, I only needed him when I was around people. If ever alone, I gladly ripped the mask off and set him aside. I hated that guy, and I wanted him away from me as much as possible.

I knew that the season I was heading into was not going to be the brightest moment in my life, but I knowingly went into it anyway.

I was heading down a path of self-destruction, and I knew it, but just didn't care.

I felt like the biggest hypocrite in the world. For the last two years, I had preached this message of freedom, authenticity, transparency, and community. God was now asking me to truly live what I had been teaching, and I said no.

How low is that?

He was just asking me to be completely authentic about who I was, but I was too scared. I didn't trust God enough, and I sure didn't trust people enough.

I sunk even lower into guilt, feeling like I had not only let God down, but I had let my students down by not obeying and living out what I believed and taught.

I would go to work during the day, but that was about as much ministry as I was doing at that point. I didn't want to be around the students. First of all, I didn't want any of them to see me like this, and secondly, I didn't want them to come to me for advice, because I was not in a place to give them the answers I was "supposed" to give.

Even my Wednesday night sermons were almost too much for me. Since God and I weren't really on speaking terms, I wasn't in a place to teach because I wasn't learning anymore. I resorted to showing lots of videos and having guest speakers during this time.

I realized the irony at that point, though. I has spent my life wishing that being gay wouldn't stop God from loving me. Then I figured out that it didn't change God's love for me, and that made me angry with God. I had a fleeting thought that maybe it wasn't being gay I was afraid of, maybe it was the reality of God's love. But, I swept those thoughts away. I didn't want to think about God right now.

I got braver, too, which made things even more scary and uneasy for me, because with bravery comes paranoia.

I started joining online sites with local gay people. The apps allowed me to talk to people and get to know the local gay community. At first, I made a point to only talk to people who were an hour or more away, so as not to compromise myself, but it quickly grew to a point that I just didn't care. I think part of me wanted to be outed because I wasn't able to do it myself. But, nonetheless, I got braver and braver to the point where I was actually allowing myself to be seen on the app by people right down the street. Part of me couldn't believe I was even doing this, but the rest of me still couldn't care less.

I was numb.

The whole month of October, I was just going through the motions of ministry and letting Straight-Face enjoy his daylight time. But at night, the mask came off, and I simply drank my pain away while talking to guys. I had withdrawn myself from my friends, my family, and especially my church.

How did it get to this? I began to ask myself.

God, You bring me on this journey, and I actually get to the point where I believe homosexuality is not a sin, and now it gets to this? I am miserable.

But I knew it was a pointless prayer. God had already let me know that He was moving ahead. The discussion was over. Besides, I knew that it really wasn't God that I was angry with, but He made an easy target. I knew that it was actually me, and the circumstance in my life, that I was truly angry with. I was miserable because I was stuck, and I was upset with myself for not having the strength and courage to do something about it. God had already told me what to do, but I was acting like Jonah and giving God my own plans. I was running. I was on the retreat, and there was no way in hell I was going to go to my own personal Ninevah.

———————————

Buzz buzz.

I reached in my pocket and grabbed my phone. My roommate and his girlfriend were on the couch, and I was in the recliner, so I knew it was safe. When you're hiding in the closet, you're phone becomes your personal holy grail. No one touches it. No one looks at it. I never even kept my phone on loud, because I didn't want people knowing when I received text messages, or anything else. It was always on vibrate.

They were engaged in the movie, so I checked it. It was a message from the gay dating app.

It was the first of November, and things had not progressed since the last month. In fact, they were probably worse because I was getting much braver. I was becoming more of a recluse, and it was quite possibly the first time I had even hung out with my roommate and his girlfriend in a while. I didn't want them seeing me talking on the app, so I stood up and went to my bedroom. That was the norm lately, so they thought nothing about it.

The message was from a guy named Wes, and it made me smile just receiving the message. We had been talking for a couple of days now, and we really clicked. He was a southern boy like myself. He liked to hunt, fish, and listen to country music. That's hard to find in another gay guy, so we were quite interested in each other from our first conversation.

"So?" his message said.

"So what?" I replied, knowing what he meant. He was referring to the fact that I had not sent him a picture of myself yet, and I could tell he was getting aggravated. I didn't blame him. But, I was still being paranoid about pictures. The app said that he was only twelve miles away, so I knew it was quite possible that he knew me. However, I was about ready to give in. I had done some Facebook stalking and knew that we didn't really know any of the same people.

"Are you going to send a picture or not?" he replied.

After a minute of thinking how to word it, I replied. "Okay… but a few things…"

"Yes?"

"I just want you to know I am majorly in the closet. That's why I've been so hesitant."

"No duh."

"Yeah, but like, my job could depend on it…" I said. There was no reply for a few minutes, as I sat on my bed and stared at the phone.

"I know it doesn't mean much, but you can trust me. I will not tell a soul."

My palms were sweating and my heart was beating faster. I attached a picture to the message, took a deep breathe and pushed send.

I fell back on the bed and held my breath until he responded. I was just waiting for him to reply, "Holy crap, you're that youth minister! I know you!"

Buzz Buzz.

I hurriedly grabbed my phone and opened the message.

"You're cute. And don't worry, I don't know you. Haha."

Outwardly, I just smiled, but inwardly, I shrieked like a junior high girl.

I really didn't know what to say. I really wanted to, but I knew that if I ever really met up with him, then that was the end of my rope. So far, this had all been theoretical. But the moment I met this guy in person, I was going to be in the "gay lifestyle" and I really didn't think there would be any return from that. So, I proposed to him that just for the time being, we simply text each other. He seemed to be okay with that. I gave him my actual phone number so that we didn't have to use the app, and we kept talking.

And talk we did.

We talked from the time I woke up until the time I went to sleep.

Of course, this didn't help my paranoia. I set a lock on my phone just in case a student or a friend grabbed it. I changed his name on my phone to make it look like he was a relative. I made sure not to text him when I was around people, and I kept my phone in my pocket at all times.

The anxiety bottled up inside of me. I tried to drink away the anxiety at night, but that didn't solve anything. It just led to hangovers.

All the secrets, all the lies, all the paranoia. I couldn't handle it much longer.

A couple of days later, I determined that it was too much to keep inside any longer. Maybe if I told someone, it could relieve a little of the stress. The first person who came to mind was Connie. She was the only person I knew I could tell, and I already knew what her reaction was going to be.

———

She was usually on Facebook chat at night because we talked quite often. That night, I waited for her to log on. I could have called her, but I wanted to do it online so that I could think about what I was saying before I said it.

She finally logged on, and I sent her a message saying hi, and she quickly replied. I was more nervous than I remember ever being. It wasn't that I was scared of her rejecting me, because I knew that would never happen. I think I was more scared of the fact that I was admitting it to someone I actually knew.

The thing about coming out is that you really can only do it to a person once. Once those words are out there, there is no going back.

But, I knew I had to do it.

"What's up?" she asked.

"Well," I replied, "I've met someone!"

My breathing was getting heavy. I couldn't believe I was doing this.

"That's wonderful!" she said.

"Yeah, this person is really cool, too."

I was working really hard to not say "he."

"So how'd you meet her?"

"Well, this person and I met online." I replied, "And they are really cute, and we have really clicked. Been talking nonstop for a while now."

"That's really cool, sweetie. I'm proud for you."

"Yeah, I'm hoping it works out with them. We will see, I guess."

She didn't respond. I was waiting for something to make this easier. I threw out hints, but it wasn't working. Finally, after a few minutes that seemed like forever, she responded.

"So are you going to tell me his name?"

Did she really just say that?

My heart turned inside my chest and my stomach dropped. I guess she did get the hint.

"How'd you know?" I wrote back.

"I could just tell by the way you were talking. You wouldn't acknowledge the gender. And it's okay, hon! So tell me about him!"

I almost burst into tears and jumped for joy at the same time. I had finally gotten the affirmation I had waited my whole life to hear. I had been thinking about this conversation since I first daydreamed about telling Mrs. Lopez so many years ago. It was happening now, and it felt amazing.

Straight-Face was slowly dying off, and I was okay with that.

Connie was talking to Brandon, the real Brandon. I had finally came out to someone I knew, and it felt good.

Really good.

After a couple of week of talking with Wes, talking was no longer enough. He wanted to meet me in person, and I knew that if I didn't meet him, he was going to get bored with me and quit talking. I really didn't want him to quit talking, either, because it was so nice to connect with somebody.

My heart skipped a beat as I finally said, "Okay, I can meet you, but you need to know something."

"What do I need to know?" he replied.

"I'm very in the closet."

"Yeah, I know. We covered this. I am, too, remember?"

"No," I replied, "I mean, I'm a minister at a church that you probably know of, and if it gets out, then I will lose my job and a lot of friends. It will be a scandal, and it will be horrible for me."

He replied that it was okay, and gave me a heartfelt promise that word would never get out, because he was in the closet himself.

I did want to see him, though, before I hung out with him. I wanted to make sure he was for real. He told me he was working, and that he worked in the mall. Little did he know that I lived right beside the mall, so I went next door and walked by his store. I saw him helping a customer.

He was beautiful! I couldn't believe he was real.

I sent him a text message and told him I just saw him at the mall, and he was upset that he didn't get to see me, so I told him I'd walk by again. I slowly took steps in front of the big plate glass window between us. I turned in his direction and our eyes locked.

I simply just smiled and nodded, and he did the same.

I kept walking, hoping he was still interested in me after seeing me in real life.

Buzz Buzz.

I grabbed my phone as fast as I could to see his text.

"OMG we have to hang out soon!" he said.

If I could have skipped through the mall without drawing attention to myself, I'm sure I would have.

So, we made plans.

———————————

Since he was in the closet, we couldn't go to his place, and we couldn't go to my place, either. We decided that we would rent a hotel room and just hang out there all night, and that would be our date because we couldn't go out.

I knew I was digging myself a hole, but I felt like I couldn't stop it.

Brandon, you have to stop this before it goes too far.

Straight-Face was grasping for straws. He knew he had lost his hold on me, but it didn't mean that he had shut up completely.

If you meet him in real life, it's game over. You're done. No more ministry for you. No going back.

This was the only thing Straight-Face could hold over my head these days. He knew that my theology of homosexuality had changed, but that didn't mean the guilt trips had stopped. He liked to remind me that just because God may be okay with homosexuality, it didn't mean that everyone else in my life was, too.

You're going to lose everything. All of the people you love are going to be done with you.

The sad part is that I knew he was right. But, I was still too pissed at God and too pissed with life in general to care enough to do anything about it. I just went with the flow, even if the current was going to pull me down and drown me. It just didn't concern me anymore.

It was now the middle of November. I finished up a Wednesday night service and quickly jetted away from the church. We had planned to meet at a parking lot on the edge of town, far from where anyone we knew could potentially see us.

I pulled into the lot and saw his car, still running, parked in a spot in the middle. I parked my car beside his. The windows were tinted so dark that I couldn't see inside. Part of me was glad, because if we took his car, no one could see me inside. The other side of me was really paranoid because I was hoping I hadn't been set up. I took a deep breath as I turned my car off and got out. I opened the passenger side door of his car, expecting the worst.

Wes was sitting in the driver's seat, and he smiled at me.

"Hop in," he said, while the radio played the local pop station.

I got inside. He could tell I was nervous.

"It's okay! Relax," he said, smiling at me. I smiled back.

"Yeah, I know it will be okay. It's still just..."

"I know," he interrupted. "You don't have to explain."

I smiled shyly.

"So, are you hungry?" he asked.

"Well, kind of. But, we really can't go to a restaurant," I laughed nervously.

"That doesn't mean we can't get drive-thru!" He was so relaxed that it made him even more attractive than he already was.

We grabbed some food, and he made a joke about our "romantic drive-thru first date." We both laughed about it, but we knew it was our only option. This is a fact that only people who have had to hide their relationships will ever understand. The little things you take for granted in a normal relationship are the biggest tasks for relationships in
the closet.

Straight-Face was in my ear, telling me to stop this while I still could.

It's not too late. You can still back out. Save yourself. Save your ministry.

I consciously ignored him, trying not to let on that he was even in my ear.

We headed towards the hotel after we grabbed our food. We talked so naturally that it wasn't even awkward, even though my heart was beating so fast I could hardly stand it.

We got inside the room, and he sat on the bed. Wes had a stack of his favorite movies that he brought for us to watch. He spread them out on the bed and asked which movie I wanted to watch.

I walked over to where he was sitting, and I couldn't handle it anymore. I had waited two decades for this moment, so I leaned in and kissed him.

I kissed him *hard.*

All of those years of repression and pushing feelings aside came gushing out in one moment as I kissed him with everything I had.

The feeling was intense.

It felt good. It felt right.

At first, he was stunned by the kiss, but he began to kiss back.

We finally stopped and he laughed as he pulled away, slowly.

"Wow," he said.

"I'm sorry, but I have waited a long, long time to do that." I said, a tad bit embarrassed.

"No, it's okay. I totally understand. I've waited a long time, too."

We started the movie and lay on the bed. But before too long, the kissing continued. We didn't have sex that night, but the temptation was definitely there. However, we did continue to kiss and cuddle. In that moment, everything went out the window.

I gave in to passion.

I gave in to my feelings.

I simply gave in.

We fell asleep, woke up the next morning, and went our separate ways.

The next day, the guilt set in, and spiraled me down further.

Not only was I pissed at God, now I was pissed at myself for actually doing the thing I said I would never do in my life. I had promised my thirteen-year-old self that I wouldn't do this, and here I was, ten years later, doing it.

To make matters worse, I could tell Wes was different that next day. I found out that he wasn't actually in the closet — he was in a long-term relationship. One day in the gay world, and I was already duped. Straight-Face had a heyday with this.

See, Brandon, homosexuality itself may not be sin, but people living the gay lifestyle sure are vile and filthy. They are all depraved and wild.

I refused to believe that all gay people were debauched, but the thoughts continued to run through my head.

I fell harder into the vodka bottle, but I didn't stop talking to guys. Even though I didn't believe homosexuality was a sin anymore, I did believe casual sex was, and I knew now that I was toeing the line.

But, I was still in a state of discontent, and at this point, I really didn't care much about sin, anyway.

After Wes, I became more cautious about talking to people too local, however. I was still protecting myself because I didn't want to be found out. I set a standard that I wouldn't talk to anyone in town, but only people from neighboring places. On the app, you could tell how far people were from you, and if they were too close, I just wouldn't talk to them.

———————————

Toward the end of November, I was in the living room with my best friend, Kirstyn. We were watching a movie when her roommate came over, and she was laughing. She cut her eyes at me, and I pretended I wasn't listening as she whispered in Kirstyn's ear.

I was scared because she looked very suspicious, and this roommate of Kirstyn's was in the band at the college, so she had lots of gay friends. I was afraid of what she may have heard.

Luckily for me, she was not a good whisperer.

She said that her gay friend was at the apartment next door, and he had an app on his iPhone for gay dating. Someone was showing up on the profile who was only a few feet away, and that meant it had to be someone around the apartment.

My heart sank.

Still pretending I wasn't paying attention, I quickly pulled out my iPhone and blocked her friend so that he couldn't see my profile anymore. I was so panicked that I could hardly contain myself. My skin was crawling and my head clouded up.

Kirstyn chimed up that she had to go, and so she and her roommate went back to their apartment next door. I was freaking out. A few minutes later, she texted me and asked, "How tall are you?"

I knew exactly what this was about. My profile on the app had me listed as five feet, eleven inches tall, and one-hundred-eighty-five pounds.

My response was quick, like I didn't even think about it: "I'm five-ten. Why?"

"No reason. We were just guessing and I thought five-ten. I'm good!" she replied back.

I sighed a sigh of relief as I sank onto the bed. I had side-stepped that one, but it confirmed that I had to be more careful. It was now obvious how easily things could change, and how close I was to ruining everything.

Chapter Seventeen

December had slipped up on me out of nowhere. It's funny how fast time flies when you stop caring about anything.

I was glad it was December, though, because youth ministry pretty much died this time of year, and so I didn't have that extra pressure of having to wear Straight-Face so often.

I decided that during December I was going to cut back on the alcohol and focus more on being healthy. If I wanted to get things on track, I had to start making better decisions. I was on the treadmill at my local gym, listening to music using my iPhone, when it dinged through the headphones. I checked the phone and saw it was a message on the gay dating app. I slowed the treadmill down to a walk and opened the app to see who it was.

He was more than a hundred miles away, and the picture he had was really cute, so I replied. He responded almost instantly.

"What's up?"

"Just at the gym at the moment. What about you?" I sent back. As I waited on his reply, I checked his profile. He was a year younger than me, and was a student at a university in Tennessee. I felt safe talking to him, since he was so far away.

"I'm just procrastinating for finals. Do you have a picture?"

This was a normal question on the app if you didn't have a picture posted. As someone in the closet, I hated when they asked me this, but he was so far away that I didn't mind. I sent him my picture.

He seemed interested in me, and we hit it off quite nicely. We continued talking as I moved on to the weight room at the gym. We kept asking basic questions back and forth, getting to know one another. Interest began to pick up between both of us.

"So, do you mind if I have your number?" he asked. "It would be easier than the app."

I didn't mind at all, since he was not a threat. I sent him the number and continued my set on curls. My headphones dinged that I had a text message, so I assumed it was from him. I waited until I finished my set, and then pulled the phone out. My heart dropped as I saw the phone number. It was a local number.

"Maybe it's not him!" I thought to myself as I opened the message.

"Hey, it's Jake!" it said. It was him. I thought I was going to pass out.

I quickly sent him a text back: "That is a local number for me?!.."

"Yeah, I'm from Jonesboro. I just go to school here." He sent back quickly.

I flipped out. I told him I was really deeply in the closet, and confessed to him that I was a minister at a local church. I needed him to understand how important it was that he didn't tell a soul.

"What church??" he asked.

I didn't want to tell him, but he finally forced it out of me. I guessed it was too late since he already had my picture and name anyway.

"No way!" he replied, "I know a lot of people there. In fact, the college minister's wife and I are really close!"

My stomach knotted up and I thought I was going to throw up. The room started spinning. I felt like I had crossed the line, and now this guy was going to be the ruin of me. But, I was already too deep in this, and I couldn't just quit talking to him now.

"Don't worry," he added. "I would never out anyone. Your secret is safe with me!"

It was a start, but I still wasn't sure I trusted him. We kept talking, though, and the more I got to know him, the more comfortable I became with him. He told me his story, and I told him mine, and we talked nonstop for the next two days.

On the third day, I awoke to a text from Jake: "I'm driving to Jonesboro tonight to see you."

"Woah! What?" I sent back as I jumped up out of bed, suddenly awake, "What about finals?"

"I'm done. My last one is today, and I'm leaving after that. I really want to see you in person."

"Okay. I'll make sure my night is free." I said, very hesitantly. He wanted me to meet him at a restaurant. I was so reluctant, but I finally agreed. The double life I was living was getting the best of me, and I was getting too tired to try anymore.

Around eight o'clock that night, I met him at the restaurant and we talked for about an hour over chips and salsa. I watched the door in paranoia, but luckily no one I knew showed up at the restaurant. We left there and went to his house to watch a movie. We were clicking, and unlike the last guy I met in person, I felt like this may actually last and could be something.

As we were watching the movie, we kissed.

He smiled at me, and then said he wanted to take it slow. I was very content with that because I wasn't ready to take any plunges, either. We laid there and watched television for a long time. It was the most peace I had felt in months.

I was finally content for a brief moment.

After that night, we kept talking. Things were different for me.

The whole experience was almost affirmation for me.

I had confidence, and I was content.

I had finally concluded that maybe — just maybe — God was right.

After more than two months of not talking to God, I finally came crawling back like the prodigal son.

I knew it was going to be a long conversation between God and me, so I went up to the church about ten o'clock at night, when I knew nobody would bother me. We had built a small prayer room in the youth area, and I went in there and closed the door.

I knelt down, and just talked to God.

God, first of all, I'm sorry. I have been nothing but rebellious towards You for a long time now. Truth is, I've been angry with You. Actually, I've been down-right pissed off at You. I thought it was unfair that You made me this way. I've been mad that You asked me to come out. I've just been mad about a lot of things. Mad at myself, mad at others, mad at the church. I think I'm finally at a point, though, where I can say yes to You. I guess if this is what You want me to do, then I'll do it. I don't understand it, but I guess I'll say yes. I'll start trying to figure out how I'm going to do this. This isn't going to be easy. Matter of fact, this is probably going to suck really badly. But if that's what You want, then okay. God, I just want to please You.

"Brandon, I'm already pleased with you."

It was the first time I had felt God's voice in a long time, and it was so enlivening to feel his presence again. But what was even more reviving was what he was saying.

"I've always been pleased with you," he continued, "even though you never knew it."

I know I've worked hard, God. I know I've got Straight-Face. I just thought that if You loved him enough, maybe some of that would rollover to make You love me too, I guess.

That's when God responded with words that would change things for the rest of my life.

"Brandon, I love all of my creation. Straight-Face, though, is your creation, not mine. I don't love Straight-Face. I love you."

I couldn't even speak. I had never felt the presence of God more in my life than in that very moment. I knew I had heard the voice of truth, and God was revealing his love for me — the real me. I just simply knelt there and basked in the presence of True Love.

Chapter Eighteen

I left the prayer room that night a changed person. I felt like I was starting to catch up to God, and it was nice to feel his presence in my life again. I knew my life was about to become a roller coaster, but I simply buckled up and hoped for the best. I felt God had brought me this far, so I just had to hold on in faith that he would hold on to me throughout the entire ride.

I started making plans for the future. I began talking to Connie about moving to Memphis and started searching for jobs in that area to support me until I figured out what I was supposed to do.
It was such a scary time, but I was rolling with it as best as I could. I had no idea how this whole "coming out" thing was going to take place. I was just hoping I did it delicately and that it was as drama-free as possible.

I was getting gutsy, though.

When I began to believe that God loved me just as I was, then that gave me more confidence to simply be myself. If God accepted me, then it was less of a concern whether other people did or not.

An old high school teacher of mine lived in the same town as I did, and she and I had stayed in touch over the years. She is a lesbian, and had recently married a woman. They were planning a Christmas get-together, and she had invited me over, as she usually did. I called her the day before the party.

"Hey, Teresa, I have a question."

"What's up?" she asked.

"Well, I was wondering if it would be okay if I brought a date to the party?"

"Well, sure! I don't mind at all."

"Okay, well, there's just one thing…" I hesitated.

"What's that?"

The next few seconds felt like a million years. She had to have noticed the pause, but I didn't practice the conversation beforehand, so I didn't know how to word it. I knew I couldn't just come right out and say it. When you're coming out, there is still a sense of not wanting to say it outright at first, because you're still so hesitant, and partly still in denial. It gets easier to say it after a few times, but those few times are the hardest. I finally figured out a way to phrase it.

"Well, this person is not exactly a…girl." I said.

She paused, and I could tell she was little shocked.

"Oh. OH!" she laughed, "Okay. Well, you know that's not a problem with me."

"Well, I know it's not a problem," I replied, "but I was making sure that no one at the party would be someone I knew personally, if you catch my drift?"

She knew I worked for an Evangelical church, and she put two and two together.

"Oh, I understand. I'm pretty sure you wouldn't know any of the same people I hang out with."

Jake and I went to the party and hung out with everyone. Many of the people there were gay or lesbian, and the rest of them were allies. It was so refreshing to be in an atmosphere where I could simply be me for a night, and be so open about my sexuality. He and I sat beside each other and even held hands a couple of times while we were there. It was a bold move for me, but I was embracing the accepting atmosphere like a cool glass of wine.

For the first time since I was fifteen, Straight-Face was completely silent. God put him to sleep, and I was finally living my own life.

———————

Jake and I kept talking the remainder of the month, but things started to fizzle. He told me that he was about to have to move to Chicago. We decided to continue as friends and move from there. We kept chatting, but kept it to a friend level.

But even though Jake was gone, I had already tasted what it was like to have some minute intimacy with someone, and after twenty-years of keeping that bottled up, it wasn't going to be pushed back that easily anymore.

My mind went back to Peej from so many years before, and how I wanted so badly to tell him that I was gay, too. It dawned on me just how far I really had come since he and I last talked back in college. I knew I had some unfinished business.

I didn't have his number anymore, so I sent him a Facebook message, just like the first time I talked to him outside of class. Luckily, he replied quickly, and we chatted back and forth for a little while, about where we were, and what was going on in our lives. Finally, I couldn't take it anymore.

"So, Peej, I do have some big news in my life, but I need it to be on the down low. How good are you at keeping secrets?" I typed.

"I'm the best. :)" He replied.

"Well, I need you to be really good at this one because it could cost me my job…"

"Oh, wow. Seriously, you know I won't tell a soul. What's up?" I tried to figure out how to phrase this.

"I wanted so badly to tell you this in college, but I just couldn't at the time. But, I've come to a place now where I'm comfortable with it," I finally mustered.

"Okay?"

I could tell the anticipation was getting to him.

"Well, I'm gay."

He didn't respond.

I waited and waited.

I had a minor freak out, with every possible scenario running through my head. After what seemed like forever, he finally responded. He was pretty much in shock, and he told me about how much he had a crush on me in college, but he always thought I was straight. I then confessed to him the crush I had on him back in the day, and how my inviting him to worship services was me actually hitting on him. We both decided I needed to work on my flirting skills.

We had such a wonderful conversation for a long time, with him finally inviting me somewhere that caught me off guard: "So, you should go to the gay club with me."

I didn't really know what to say. I had never even been to a straight club, much less a gay one. Plus, what if someone saw me?! This was my biggest concern.

"Eh, I don't know, man. What if someone from my church sees me there?" I replied back.

"If someone from your church sees you there, then they'll probably be just as scared to see you as you are of them."

He made sense. If I saw someone there that I knew, then that just meant they were living with a mask just like I had been. So, after much persuasion, he finally talked me into it.

The club was in Memphis, so I traveled over on Friday and spent the night with Connie. Peej and three of his friends all met me in Memphis that next Saturday night to go eat. That was the first time I ever really just hung out with gay people, and I felt like I did the first night I went with the youth group to eat pizza. I felt foreign, but also felt like I belonged. I knew it took me a while to adjust to living within Evangelicalism, so I had patience because I knew it was going to take some adjusting here, as well.

It was also the first time that I went out in public without Straight-Face on, other than Teresa's party. But even that didn't feel public because we were at least in the confines of someone's house. We were in a city an hour and a half away from my church, so even though I was on edge, it wasn't quite as bad. I started relaxing as I hung out with Peej and his friends. One of his friends, Ashley, and I hit it off really well. She had a similar religious background and had recently come out as well. We all had a blast at the restaurant, but then the time had come. It was time for the club.

I really didn't know what to expect. I was scared and excited, hesitant and anxious. Both of my identities were shaking, but for different reasons. I was shaking for anticipation; Straight-Face, well, he was just nervous as hell.

As we stood in line waiting to get in, I could hear the bass pumping loudly. There were lights beaming out of the front door. I saw men hanging all over other men, women all over other women. A drag queen walked past me and went inside. It was the first time I saw a drag queen in person, and you would have thought I just saw an alien from Jupiter. I think Peej picked up on my anxieties. He leaned in toward me and laughed.

"It's going to be okay. Nobody is going to see you. You're going to be fine!" He whispered as he took my hand and patted me on the back.

I breathed deeply and exhaled.

"You're right. I'm just not going to worry about it, and I'm going to have fun," I said. I was really telling this to myself more than I was to him.

We paid our cover charge and walked through the door.

The bass.

That's what I remember most about the first moment I walked into the club.

The bass was thumping so loudly, I could feel it in my chest. It was like an extra heart beating in sync with my own.

I could feel it pounding against my ears, against my chest, against my head. The vibrations ran through my veins and throughout my body. It simply took over.

I passed the entrance and my eyes adjusted. The lights were shooting all over the place, but somehow the whole place was really dark. There were men running around without their shirts on, and women with crew-cut haircuts going the other way. In the middle of the room was a stage with a huge pole stretching all the way to the ceiling. There was a young guy around my age with nothing but underwear on hanging upside down on the pole as a small crowd of people threw dollar bills at him.

The bass kept pumping, but I think my heart was outrunning it. I soaked it all in, not knowing whether to be horrified or enamored.

Finally, Peej snapped me out of it as he pulled me up to the bar.

"What do you like to drink?" He asked.

"Umm, anything with vodka."

"Red bull and vodka," he said as he turned toward the bartender.

In a few moments, all of us had drinks in our hands, and we held them up together.

"To Brandon's first club visit!" Peej exclaimed as we all tapped our plastic cups together before downing them.

We were now in a different room with Dubstep music blaring louder than before. There was a disco ball hanging from the ceiling and laser lights shooting in every direction. This room was a huge auditorium with a large stage and dance floor.

Peej could tell that I was wondering what the purpose of this room was.

"This is where they have the drag show," he yelled at me over the blaring music.

"That's cool!" I said.

It was all I knew to say. I had never been to a drag show before. Hell, I just saw my first drag queen a few minutes before. Everything was happening so fast, I really didn't have much to say. I was just trying to figure out what was going on around me.

The rest of the crew said they were going to go dance, but Peej said he was going to stay back with me for a few minutes.

"You doing okay?" he asked. I could tell by his voice that he was genuine. He truly just wanted me to have a good time. In that moment, I knew I had a friend in Peej.

"Yeah, I'm good. Just soaking it all in."

"It's a little crazy your first time," he said as he laughed, "but you'll get the hang of it."

"Yeah, I'm sure I will," I said, smiling.

I wasn't so sure, though. This was definitely not my element. I much preferred a night at home with friends than the craziness of a club. But, I felt I should at least try my best to embrace it. I needed to at least give it a shot.

"You want to go dance?" He finally asked as a song came on that was one of his favorites.

I figured the vodka had kicked in well enough by this point that maybe I could loosen up on the floor, so I agreed. He took my hand and led me to the crowded dance floor. We found a niche in the crowd and started dancing.

It came about naturally, but also very awkwardly. I had never danced with another guy before without it being a joke. But Peej grabbed me in close and started swaying back and forth with the beat. I followed suit, and before I knew it, I didn't even notice the awkwardness. I was just having fun. We danced for a couple of songs, then met with the rest of the crew back at the bar where we all sat around and chatted for a bit.

I watched the crowd a lot during that time. I watched these openly gay men and women walk around with their friends, and I felt connected. We all had something in common. We all knew the struggles that came with our feelings. I wondered how many of them grew up religious or still believed God hated them for who they are attracted to. My heart hurt for some of them as I watched them, because I could see the hurt and rejection on their faces.

A lot of times, you can tell who has been rejected and hurt by their families and friends when they came out. These are the ones, a lot of times, who end up trying to drink or smoke their pain away. I'm not making a blanket statement. Not every gay person who is rejected ends up hurting themselves in this way, but a lot of the times, the ones that are hurting themselves are ones who have been rejected by those they love. And a lot of times, these are the same ones who feel God has rejected them, as well.

I kept studying the room, wondering who had their own Straight-Faces, and who had already killed their masks off. I envied a lot of them, but mostly, I just enjoyed being there in that place, surrounded by an environment where I was safe. By the time I snapped out of my daydream, I realized my friends had gone back to the dance floor, and it was just me and Peej standing there. He smiled at me. I smiled back.

Next thing I knew, he leaned in and kissed me. It lasted for a little while and ended in both of us giggling.

"I've wanted to do that since freshman year," he says.

"Yeah, well, I've wanted you to do that since freshman year."

He laughs.

I look up to Ashley giving me a thumbs up from the dance floor, then inviting us both over.

"I guess we better go dance," I said as I turned to Peej, smiling again.

"Well, let's do this!"

We danced the night away, all of us just enjoying each other's company in a place where we didn't have to hide anything. We were being real, and we were having fun. On that night, all was right in the world, and on the way home, I knew that it was time to pull the plug on the life-support of Straight-Face. It was time for him to go.

———————————

I wanted to come clean with my brother. I figured his gaydar had already gone off on me, but I had to actually say it. He deserved that much. He lived eight hours away, so I called him on the phone one day while I was driving home from work.

"Hey, bubba, I need to talk to you about something," I said, trying to not sound too serious, but I knew I did.

"You can talk to me about anything. What's up?" he replied.

"Well, I think you may already know this," I started. I knew with him I couldn't beat around the bush. He deserved me just saying it out right, so I added, "I'm pretty sure I'm gay."

"Yeah," he laughed, "I kind of picked up on that, but I was going to wait until you told me."

"Well, I appreciate that."

I truly did. Nothing good comes from forcing people out of the closet. It is best to let them tell you in their own time, in their own way. I was so glad my brother was wise enough to let me do it this way.

"So, have you told anyone else in the family?" he asked.

"Not yet, but I am planning on telling mom really soon."

We chatted for a couple of hours while I drove around. There was no way I could go home because my roommate would hear me. I drove aimlessly around Jonesboro while he gave me advice that he had learned over the years since he came out.

In that moment, I realized how blessed I was to have a big brother to go to, and especially blessed that we had become so close. Most gay guys with older brothers just don't understand each other;

199

they spend a lot of time trying to figure each other out because they're both so different. But I was blessed. I had a brother who truly understood what it was like for me, and he was willing to share his experiences.

As I hung up the phone after the long conversation, I thanked God for my older brother.

———————————

I knew the next person I had to tell was my mom. I knew she would be okay with it because she had thrown me hints for a while. Somehow, I always knew that my mom knew. I chalked it up to mother's intuition. But she wasn't going to ask me about it right out, either.

I called her on the phone a couple of days after I told my brother. I told her I had gone to Teresa's party and that it was fun. She worked at the school while I was growing up, so she knew Teresa, and that she was a lesbian. That was my first hint. I told her I had been talking to Teresa and her new wife quite a bit lately. I followed that up with my thoughts about moving to Memphis, working my way toward telling her.

Finally, after beating around the bush, I just came out and said it: "Mom, you know I'm gay, right?"

She laughed and simply responded, "It's about fucking time you told me."

I laughed, too.

I really laughed.

The moment was so surreal for me. It was finally out there with my mom, the lady who I loved so deeply. I didn't have to hide it from her at all anymore.

We talked for a long time that day. I told her stories about my struggle growing up, about how my theology had changed, and what I thought God was calling me to do.

She shared stories, too, about the times that she thought maybe I had been gay, and what made her feel that way.

We connected deeply that night.

Brandon finally got to talk to his momma.

———————————————

So, that was one parent down, and one more to go. Although, the second one was not going to be so easy. As a matter of fact, I was terrified.

Dad was different.

I knew that Dad knew, too, or at least suspected it. We had thrown hints before, but mom relayed that he had always chalked it up to a phase during teenage years. After the girlfriends through college, he thought I had gotten past that phase.

My dad and I have always been very close. He's not only my dad; he's one of my best friends. I saw how it affected my brother's and his relationship when he came out, and I didn't want it to affect ours like that.

After my brother came out, they didn't talk for almost three years. My dad had a cancer scare, though, that caused him to do a re-evaluation of everything, and in that process, he came to terms with my brother's homosexuality, and they mended their relationship. Even though he and my brother finally got past it, I knew that it was still a possibility that it could damage our relationship, and that scared me. I really had no clue how I was going to do it, either. I thought I would probably postpone this one for a little while.

Finally, I decided that I would wait until I was in a serious relationship before I told him.

Christmas had come and gone, and another new year was approaching. I had no plans for New Years Eve, and my friends didn't either. My dad called and said he was going to be home that night, and my group of friends and I should come to his house and let him host New Year's for us. He and mom had finalized the divorce, and I knew it would be good for him for us to go and hang with him that night.

Plus, he said he would buy the drinks for us, and so that definitely sold my friends.

So, Kirstyn, Jimmy, and I, along with the rest of Kehila, took a road trip to my dad's house that night and arrived at about 9 o'clock. It was pretty cool to have my dad hang with my friends, and we were having a blast.

As the night rolled on, Dad was making our drinks, and we were enjoying the company of everyone. However, after a few drinks in, he mentioned he wasn't using vodka in these drinks. He was using 100 percent pure grain alcohol.

Uh-oh.

Before I knew it, I had blacked out. It was the only time I have ever blacked out because I had always been pretty responsible with how much I was drinking. But, this time I had no control over it.

About an hour and a half later, I came to, as I was coming out to my dad. I was sitting at the dining room table, and he was hugging me, and smiling at me. When I came to, the first thing I heard was: "You are my son, and I love you for who you are, and I support you in whatever you do. Nothing will ever change that."

It was like hearing the audible voice of God.

As weird as this sounds, I believe God used that drunken mistake for his purpose. I know that I probably would have waited a long time to tell my dad; but instead, I got this glorious moment of getting it all out in the open and getting to hear my dad say the words that every gay person wants to hear from their parents.

My dad hugged me and then went back to the other room. I pulled out my phone and sent a text to my brother: "I just came out to dad. It went great!"

I pushed send, then my heart dropped.

I noticed that I didn't send it to my brother, I sent it to my best friend, Kirstyn, whose name happened to be right below my brothers.

She was sitting in the same room at the party. I was literally looking at her!

I knew there was no going back now. I watched as she pulled out her phone. I saw the look of confusion on her face. She raised her eyebrows at me from across the house and raised her hands in the air, as a way to tell me she was confused.

I looked at her and motioned for her to come over to the kitchen table where I was still sitting, because there were less people there. She came over, still looking confused.

"What are you talking about?" she asked.

"Kirstyn, I'm five foot, eleven," I said.

She was still very confused.

"I'm five foot, eleven, Kirstyn." I repeated.

She sat for a second, letting it sink in. Then, she remembered the night I told her I was five-ten to get her off my trail.

Finally, it hit her.

Then she hit me, really hard on the arm.

"You lied to me!" she said. I could tell she wasn't really angry. It made me laugh, and I needed to laugh.

"I'm sorry!" I said.

"It's okay. You know that's okay. You're my best friend. I love you."

Telling family and telling friends that you are gay are two completely different experiences. When you tell family, and they take it horribly, you're still family. A lot of times, they do come around, even if it takes a long time. Even if they take it horribly, you assume they still love you even if they don't approve of who you are or your decision to be real about it.

Friends, however, don't have to be your friends. Often, your biggest fear in coming out is that your friends are going to abandon you and not want anything to do with you. The worst fear of coming out is realizing the possibility of loneliness. Even though I knew my friends thought a lot like I did, there was still a real fear that things would be just too weird between us after that.

So, when Kirstyn said what she did, all I could do was hug her. That hug meant more than she'll ever know. It was a hug of gratitude, thanking her for standing by my side, and for not hating me. It was a hug of appreciation, for being such a great friend. It was a hug of love, because I knew our friendship bonded that night in a new and special way, and that we were going to be friends for a long, long time.

Chapter Nineteen

We made it through New Years Eve, and our designated drivers got us back home that night. Unfortunately, New Years day was on a Sunday, so we all had to be up for church the next morning.

In our defense, we weren't the only group dragging in that Sunday morning. Apparently, we weren't the only Baptists in the world who didn't think alcohol was such a horrible thing.

That Sunday marked a new life for me, though. I knew that everything was different, and at that point, there was no going back. While I sat through the sermon, I just prayed.

I thanked God for my family, and for the way they loved me.

I thanked God for Kirstyn, and that she was my friend. I thanked Him for His grace, for loving me, and calling me His child. I prayed that He would let me know what was next, because I had no idea.

I knew I wasn't going to stay where I was at very much longer, though. Just sitting in that sanctuary made my skin crawl.

Don't get me wrong; nothing about my students had changed. I loved those kids, and still do. But, I just didn't agree with the church anymore on hardly anything. Just about everything the pastor was saying was either bigotry or antithetical to everything I had come to believe, and it bothered me to be a part of it. The Spirit had led me on a journey that completely changed everything I believed in, thought was true, and applied to my life.

God had gone from a guy in the sky who was ready to strike me down for one little mess up, to a loving Father who, when I fell down, picked me up, patted the dust off, and smiled as He said, "So, did you learn anything from that?"

Jesus had gone from a right-wing Republican who was preaching moralism to a crazy hippie who taught about grace for everyone, love for all, and simply serving others in the name of God, the Father.

The Spirit had gone from some theoretical entity to a real, living being who was shaping me, transforming me, and speaking to my own spirit.

The traditional church, in my mind, had gone from being the thing that leads you to God, to the place that was keeping people from truly interacting with Him and experiencing His love.

The Bible had turned from a rulebook into an amazing story of love and redemption, reconciliation and grace.

I had come a long way, and I didn't want to go back.

But what was next?

I think the worst part about following Jesus – and I mean, really following Jesus, where you have to step out on blind faith and just close your eyes, hoping He will catch you – is that you really don't know if He will catch you or not. That's why it's called faith. You aren't certain about anything. You just pray for the best.

And for me, not knowing what was next was the worst.

I've always had a plan, and I always knew what the next step was going to be throughout my whole life. Now, there was nothing there. It was just all gray, with no clear vision. I knew Memphis was probably my next move, but even that was clouded with mystery. It was possible I could live with my brother in Indiana, but since my parents had recently divorced, I didn't want to move that far away from them. In Memphis, I had Connie and the other Outlaw Preachers who lived there, who would definitely be a good support system, but I also had no job there. Connie and I had talked about doing ministry together in Memphis, but it wasn't a job. It would not pay any money. It would just simply be volunteer ministry. So, I just kept praying.

———————

That week, though, I got a phone call from a job I had applied for in Memphis. They said they wanted to meet me and talk to me. I took a day off of work and drove over for an interview, where they offered me a job. It was just a job at a restaurant, and it was not anything glorious. But it was a job.

I prayed over it and came to the conclusion that this was what I was supposed to do. Now came the hard part: pulling the plug.

I decided since I had a job secured, and that I really had nothing left to lose except my pride, it was time to tell my close friends in Kehila.

Throughout that week, I went to them one by one, saving my roommate and his girlfriend for last. Each time I told one of them, I was met with the same response: "I love you."

Honestly, it was becoming addicting.

Once you've hidden your true self long enough, thinking that people are going to hate the real you, you begin to become enamored with the fact that there are people out there who truly love you for who you are. There is no feeling that can compare with that.

I had one more person I knew I needed to tell, and this one had the most potential to get ugly. I had to tell Jeremy, the college minister, who got me the job in the first place, and who I had become such good friends with over the past few years. We worked alongside each other around three to four days a week, and he had become like an older brother to me. He had been having some problems within his family and was planning on leaving the church as well.

I asked him to meet me at a Mexican restaurant that we went to about once a week to chat. We got some chips and dip, and I asked him how he was doing. I could tell that he was going through a lot of pain of his own. We talked about his family and his situation. He asked me how I was doing, and I told him I was surviving. I told him about the job offer in Memphis and that I was going to take it, and he understood. Even though he didn't know the whole story, he knew that I was unhappy at the church, and that I couldn't stay there much longer. I looked around the restaurant. This is the same restaurant Jake met me at when he came home from college to see me. My mind reeled. The past few months had taken me so far already.

After a brief period of silence, I finally got up my courage.

"So, I know you have a lot going on right now, and you don't need anymore drama, but I feel like I have to tell you something, as a friend," I said.

"What's up, man? What's wrong?" He asked as he perked up in his seat. I didn't want to prolong this because with all that was going on with his life, his imagination was probably already running wild.

"I'm going to blow your mind for a second, and I hope that's okay."

"Okay?" He said, his curiosity growing.

"Well, man, I'm gay."

He sat there for a second.

"Wow," he replied.

"Yeah. I've always known, and God has called me to come clean about it. I'm not sure why He's doing that, but that's what He's doing. I can't keep it bottled up anymore."

I was so nervous I was shaking. I ate a chip to try and ease the moment. I explained a little bit about my story to him, and that my hope was that in the future, I could help gay people who were just trying to make sense of the world. I felt called to help merge sexuality and faith.

I looked up and there was a tear streaming down his face. I froze, not knowing what to make of that.

"Over the last couple of years, you have become almost like a son to me, and I want you to know that you are loved. You and I have gone through a lot together, and I know your heart. I know you are just following the Spirit, and for that, I support you."

Now I had a tear of my own running down my cheek. To have his approval and support meant more than I think he will ever know. We sat there and exchanged stories for a good couple of hours, and then as we left, he hugged me and reaffirmed his love and support for me. It was an unreal moment to say the least.

All of the anxiety I used to live with began to just fall off of me. The anxiety attacks were no longer there, and my stress breakouts had ceased. A heavy weight was lifted off of me by the end of that week, because all the people who were dearest to me knew the real Brandon Wallace, and none of them ceased loving me.

It was very empowering. My dad said to me, "All of those that matter to you don't mind. And so if anyone at this point minds, then they don't matter." I think he had ripped Dr. Seuss off without knowing it, but nonetheless, it rang true for me.

The new Brandon was ready to grab life by the horns and begin to actually live. Months before, God called me out of my religion in order to follow Jesus, and now I was finally taking those first steps.

Chapter Twenty

I sat down in my pastor's office and stared across the desk at him. I was nervous, although I'm not sure why. I had mixed feelings about him by this point. He was known to be vehemently against homosexuality. It was one of his most popular topics of choice and was mentioned in a sermon at least once a month.

I admired him for standing unwaveringly to his convictions; I just didn't agree with his convictions, and in my mind, his convictions were the type that was leading to so many gay teenage suicides and depression in so many homosexual people. I felt like what he called love is what I called hate. Although, in his eyes, what I called love, he called leading people to Hell. So, it was about even.

One thing I can say about the conservative world — because I've been a part of it for a long time — is that most of them aren't bad people; they're just ignorant. They are truly simply standing for what they believe in, and they believe they have every right to do that, even if what they stand for is hurtful to so many people. But it still doesn't make them bad people.

I didn't hate, or even have ill will, towards my pastor at the time I sat down at his desk. I just simply disagreed.

"Well, sir, I feel like God is calling me away from here, to help with a startup ministry in Memphis," I finally said.

He seemed shocked.

"Oh?" he said.

"Yes, sir. I've felt this way for a while, and I have done much praying about it, and I feel like it's time."

He asked if there were problems at the church, or if money was the reason behind my decision. I assured him it was neither, and that I was simply doing what God called me to do. I didn't feel led to come out to him at his point. I figured that would do more harm than good. I figured the best thing to do would be to just slip away from the church without causing any drama and disappear to Memphis.

That Wednesday, I told my students of my decision. This was the hardest thing of all. I knew I was going to miss those kids so much, but I had to step out and go where God wanted me to go.

Met with tearful eyes, I explained to them that sometimes God calls us out of where we are, so that He can do something bigger and better with us. I reiterated, though, to never take their eyes off of grace and the true message of Jesus Christ, which is wrapped in love.

They threw me a going away party that next week, and a lot of people showed up from within the church. They were there to celebrate my time there and to send me off to do a new work. For me, though, it was a funeral. It was the death of an identity and a birth of a new one. Straight-Face had died, and this was the service dropping him in the grave. I couldn't be happier about that. One verse kept running through my head that day: "Therefore, if anyone is in Christ, he is a new creation." (2 Cor. 5:17, NKJV)

That's what I felt like, too. I felt brand new.

I didn't realize just how much I had let religion run my life and let it snuff out the Spirit. My religion was quickly dying, but my spirituality was growing in new and exciting ways.

After the party, I went back to my apartment and finished packing up my stuff. Connie came the next day, and we began the move to Memphis. I remember settling into my new bedroom in Memphis for the first time. It was eerily comforting. Everything was brand new.

This was the first time I had ever lived outside of my home state. It was the first time since I could even remember that I didn't have a church home. It was the first time I didn't have a plan for my future or know what the next day was going to look like. It was all exciting and disturbing at the same time.

Just as I was getting settled in, I got a message from one of my old youth about a situation at his school.

A kid who was openly gay had performed a Lady Gaga song at the talent show just the week before, in which at the end of the song, he took off his jacket to reveal a rainbow t-shirt underneath. Well, some conservatives in the community got really bent out of shape about this. One particular lady wrote a letter to the editor about how ashamed of the school district she was, and she really lit into this high-school senior.

The students, however, did not feel the same way.

They began to backup their fellow student and stand up for him, even when the adults were running him down. A handful of my old youth were leading the charge, and it really made me proud of them. The former youth who sent me the message wanted to know if I could get ahold of some rainbow ribbons for him to pass out at school, to show support for the kid. It just so happened that Connie had some ribbons, and this kid was going to be in Memphis the next day, so we got him the ribbons. He took them to school and passed them out.

Well, needless to say, this caused a little more of a ruckus than we had intended.

Now, to this day, I'm not sure what went down between this moment and the next morning, but somehow, I was outed at the church I had just left two days before. I don't know if it was simply on speculation because of helping this kid, or if someone I had told finally talked, or if they had the CIA run my computer history. I just don't know!

All I know is that all of a sudden, I was getting message after message, phone call after phone call, and these messages were not well received.

Some of them were even quite threatening. I was told that one of my friends' dad had "better not see me out on the street."

Other times, I got a lot of "I'm very disappointed in your choice to be gay."

Sometimes I just got the simple, "I'm praying for your soul."

Talk about ripping off the band-aid! The messages just continued to pour in — some minor, others hateful, and others were downright threatening.

I was not expecting to officially come out for months down the road. I was hoping to sort of just disconnect myself from the church altogether, get my head together, let some wounds heal, and then do it.

But, it looked like God had different plans, because it was all unfolding right before me.

———————

I never knew how much you could literally feel someone's hatred.

Up to this point I had lived life through Straight-Face. He had helped make sure everyone liked me and "loved" me. My whole life was about being who others wanted me to be to please them. I had never had to deal with hatred such as this.

And it hurts.

To hear that someone thinks you, as a person, are the spawn of the devil and deception, and to hear that they hope bad things happen to you, is just too disheartening.

I even got word that my old pastor had told someone, "I hope he goes to Memphis and never comes back." This is the last thing I've ever heard from him to this day.

All of the same people who just days before were celebrating my ministry there, were now saying they "wished I had never been a part of this church, and that they never knew me."

Every message stung, and every message was like a punch to the stomach.

After enough punches to the stomach, it began to be hard to breathe.

But I knew from the start that this was going to be part of it.

Jesus said that if you make a stand for Him and for love, that you would be persecuted, and those words were beginning to become true. I was making a stand for what I believed in, and the religious people did not like it one bit.

I was clinging to many of David's psalms during this time, when he wrote about the people who hated him, and they were comforting in some tough nights.

I can't say all of the messages were bad, though. I had a lot of "secret supporters" within the church. Most of these were my old students, but some were students parents and other adults in the church. I received a lot of messages from them telling me to keep my head up and that they loved me and totally supported me.

One point of advice I can give to any straight person: if you know someone who recently came out, especially if that person is around a lot of conservative, religious people, affirm to them how much you love them, because I can promise you, that person has received a lot of these same hateful messages.

I knew for my own sanity, I had to try and control the amount of messages I was getting, though. I weeded through my Facebook friends, and I changed phone numbers. This helped some, but not entirely. My biggest problem was that I wasn't entirely moved out of Jonesboro yet, and had to make a trip back there to get the rest of my stuff. But after some of the threats, I didn't want to go alone. That's when Connie and I snuck back in at midnight to get the remainder of my things, and then I got the heck out of Dodge.

Everything was pretty shaky for about two weeks. The messages were coming in only two or three times a day by that point, and my heart was beginning to harden a little bit. I was beginning to be able to breathe again.

I settled in to my new job and in my new life in Memphis.

That's when I got another message, but this time it was different.

It was from someone in Jonesboro who was part of the gay community. He told me that there were plenty of LGBT people in Jonesboro who wanted to worship, but they had nowhere to go. They wanted to know if Connie and I would come back to Jonesboro on Sundays and lead a Bible study for them.

After some prayer and thought, we decided to do this. The Episcopal church in town offered to let us use their building, and so that next month, we began a Bible study with open doors.

We had our first worship service, and it went so great. The Spirit was definitely present with us as a group, and everything flowed so naturally.

In that room was a lot of hurt.

There were people who had been kicked out of their churches – and sometimes families – because of who they were. There were others who simply left their churches because they couldn't stand the bigotry and hatred, and they knew that was not the message of Jesus Christ.

Others came out of curiosity, and some came because they were supporting other people.

It was an eclectic group, from all kinds of backgrounds.

But we were all there worshipping the same God and singing the same songs together. It was beautiful.

As I sat there, I looked around the room.

I didn't know what God had in store for me next. I wasn't sure where I was going to go from here, or what life was going to look like for me. Everything was a veiled mystery, and all I could do was focus on living for God in the present.

He had called me out of my religious background, just so I could follow Him. Life was marching on, as I was following the Spirit, and I knew He was calling other people to do the same thing.

I kept studying the people in the room, listening to everyone sing "Amazing Grace" in unison.

That's when God whispered in my ear, "It's about time you caught up, son. Wait until you see what's next!"

Brandon Wallace,

a teacher, speaker and author based out of Memphis, Tennessee, tries to push the envelope on what it means to be a follower of Christ. His push towards authentic living and true community helps engage readers and listeners in a whole new way of experiencing spirituality and life.

Contact Info

For more information about Brandon Wallace, or to contact him about speaking engagements, you can follow him at his blog:

thegaychristian.com

CPSIA information can be obtained at www.ICGtesting.com
Printed in the USA
LVOW11s0602231214

420068LV00004B/179/P